Retribution. . .

The moment Cuchillo recognized the hated Pinner, he instinctively fisted a hand around the handle of the golden knife at the base of his spine. Now, as he heard the familiar voice of his sworn enemy, he half drew the cinqueda from its resting place.

The Apache warrior continued to watch the horsesoldier, finding room in his heart and mind to admire the man as well as hate him. Once, long ago, Cuchillo had considered Pinner a coward. And his opinion had not altered for a long time after the murder of his wife, Chipeta, and their baby son, a time when the depth of the Apache's hatred allowed no opportunity for calm and collected thought about the man.

Then he had seen Pinner. Several times. Each time failing to achieve his aim of killing the man. Each time, too, gaining a new degree of respect for him. Pinner was a bully, an intolerant tyrant of the worst kind. And, Cuchillo realized, he had mistakenly read such a trait as inevitably being the aspect of a coward's personality. For Captain Cyrus L. Pinner had proved his bravery on a number of occasions—in much the same way as he had handled the panic of the posse a few moments before.

Which pleased Cuchillo Oro. To an Apache warrior there was far greater honor in killing a man of great courage than a craven coward.

THE APACHE SERIES:

by William M. James

Apache

#13
THE BEST MAN

PINNACLE BOOKS • LOS ANGELES

APACHE #13: THE BEST MAN

Copyright © 1979 by William M. James

An original Pinnacle Books edition, published for the first time anywhere.

First printing, March 1979

ISBN: 0-523-40356-9

Cover illustration by John Alvin

Printed in the United States of America

PINNACLE BOOKS, INC.
2029 Century Park East
Los Angeles, California 90067

for Gaye Tardy—
who now knows why Cuchillo
is such a smooth guy in
one respect.

CHAPTER ONE

Cuchillo Oro pushed open the wooden shutters and looked out through the glassless window at the main street of Tyler Creek. He blinked several times against the harsh sunlight of the New Mexico morning and this helped him to bring the scene into sharper focus. But it did nothing to ease the dull ache that seemed to be caused by his skull contracting to squeeze in on his brain. He sucked saliva up from his throat and swilled it around in his mouth. But when he had spit it out over the window ledge his gums were as arid as before and the foul taste continued to coat his tongue.

"Was it worth it?" he muttered softly in his native Apache language. Then grinned out at the town, which was beginning to show the first signs of waking to greet the new day. "Sure it was, you crazy, hungover Mimbrenos," he growled, almost good-naturedly, in heavily accented English.

For awhile he remained at the window, leaning forward with his hands on the ledge, the grin fading to be replaced by an expression of deep-seated bitterness as he continued to study the dusty length of Center Street and to contemplate the futile reason he had got drunk.

He was tall for an Apache—six feet, two inches—

1

and had a fine build, nurtured and developed to a peak of physical fitness that would be envied by the vast majority of Apache braves of his age who had chosen, or had been forced, to remain on the rancherias of the Southwest. His age was, in fact, twenty-two, and at first glance a casual observer might well suppose this from the broad chest, the narrow waist with no suggestion of belly bulge, and the muscular arms and legs of the man. But a first impression would not take too much account of the face—merely see it as a number of features contributing to a whole that was handsome in the Apache way. Narrow eyes with coal black pupils, high cheekbones flanking a classically shaped nose with flared nostrils, a wide mouth above a resolute jaw—all this in a frame of thick hair, which reached to his shoulders, as dark as the eyes.

Upon closer study, Cuchillo Oro appeared older than his years, never more so than in his present frame of mind as he silently surveyed yet another blot placed by the White Eyes upon the homeland of the Apache nation. For bitterness deepened the furrows scored across the bronzed skin of his face. It also pulled his mouth into a twisted line and triggered a dull, dangerous light in his eyes. Such an expression added countless years to the age of the Apache brave, because it emanated from a depth of feeling not normally possible in one so young.

But, by his own rules, anything was possible to Cuchillo Oro, and anyone with the inclination and the perception to give the Apache more than a passing glance would likely decide that this was an Indian who had suffered more than most—had probably endured a far greater share of life's harsher experiences than many men of his own and other races who had twice or three times the number of years behind them. For how else had he developed such a vast capacity for hatred?

It required only a slight inclination and no perception at all to pinpoint one aspect of the Apache's suffering in the not-too-distant past. For he had a crippled right hand, the index and middle fingers missing, and from the attitude of the two remaining fingers and the thumb it was obvious they were virtually paralyzed.

As the Apache straightened from the window, his expression becoming composed, he used the knuckles of the mutilated hand to wipe the grit of sleep from his eyes. With his good hand he drew from the waistband of his cotton pants the golden knife from which he had derived his Spanish name, and smiled as he examined it, turning it over and over in the sunlight that shafted in through the window.

It was an unusual weapon for an Apache brave to possess. A finely made dagger of Italian origin known as a cinquedea. Fashioned in the fifteenth century, it had a double-edged blade with a needle-sharp point. Its hilt was of solid gold, studded with precious jewels. The contour handle was of ivory. Despite such adornments, the knife was perfectly balanced for either stabbing or throwing.

Since he had gained the knife—some said stolen it—it had become his most prized possession, the value he placed upon it completely unconnected with its material worth. It was simply that the golden knife—the cuchillo oro—personified the sole purpose to his life. Which was to survive for as long as it took him to track down and kill the rightful owner of the cinquedea—the hated horsesoldier who had caused this Apache to be known far and wide as "Pinner's Indian."

"Hey, redskin! Get your stinkin' ass outta bed and start in to clean up this crummy joint!"

Far and wide did not include the border town of Tyler Creek, for which the Apache was most grateful, and there were very few events in the life of Cuchillo Oro that aroused a feeling of appreciation within him.

"I will be but a short time, Señor Cabello!" he called, and was as good as his word.

Hurriedly, he replaced the knife in the sheath at the small of his back and shrugged into the loose-fitting cotton shirt, as sweat-stained and dirt-streaked as the pants. He put on his worn moccasins and the black headband that served to keep his hair off his forehead and out of his eyes. Then he stepped out of the spartanly furnished, ten-by-ten room that had been his refuge from humiliation for the three weeks he had been in town.

The door opened onto a short hallway, which dead-ended to the right and to the left was curtailed by an archway hung with strands of beads. The hallway smelled of yesterday's cooking, for the doorless entrance to the kitchen was immediately opposite Cuchillo's room. As he pushed through the curtain of beads at the archway his nostrils were assaulted by the malodorous atmosphere of the barroom of the Conquistador Cantina—tobacco smoke, spilled liquor and the sweat of men's bodies. All of these foul smells contributed to an unwanted memory of yesterday and the many days before.

4

But Cuchillo did not grimace or even wrinkle his nostrils as he stepped out into the frugally furnished barroom, and this was not just because, as an Apache living under the domination of the White Eyes, he was familiar with the stench of squalor. On this occasion, as on every other morning he had awakened in his tiny room off the cantina, the prime reason for his lack of response to his disagreeable surroundings was that he knew he shared a portion of the blame.

"Jesus, you look as bad as I feel," the owner of the Conquistador growled. Then snorted. "But that don't make me feel no better, redskin."

Cabello glowered at Cuchillo, who responded with a noncommital shrug, which was as close as the two men ever came to showing their true feelings for each other—their gestures tacitly expressed a mutual disrespect, with which both had come easily to terms.

The Apache began work at once, first clearing the bartop and half a dozen tables of the debris left by the last patrons to leave the place the previous evening. Empty bottles, glasses that were not all empty and heaps of crusted-up cigarette and cheroot stubs. Next he wiped down all the surfaces he had cleared, emptied the spittoons, swept the floor of old sawdust and scattered fresh in its place. The light was murky, because the door and window shutters had not yet been opened. But Cuchillo had performed these menial chores so many times now, he could have carried them out blindfolded. Perhaps a man without a hangover might have found the oppressive heat more uncomfortable than the half-light, but not so the Apache. For, as he worked, he sweated, and it seemed to

5

him that each bead of salt moisture squeezed from his pores carried with it a tiny grain of the liquor he had consumed the previous night. And thus were the bad effects of his drinking gradually diminished as he worked conscientiously to achieve a higher standard of cleanliness than Cabello demanded.

The owner of the cantina remained in the barroom while the Apache worked, but paid no attention to him. He sat on a high stool at one end of the bar, which stretched along the rear wall of the room, shoulders hunched and chin resting on the cupped palms of his hands as he studied an ancient and tattered elementary-school primer designed to teach children the rudiments of reading English. From time to time he unbent an elbow to raise a tall glass to his lips and sip at warm, flat sarsaparilla.

Edward Cabello was a Mexican-American who had late in life undertaken to learn to read the English language, which he now spoke better than Spanish. He was sixty-five and looked ten years older, mainly because he drank too much and did not eat enough. He was six feet tall and emaciated—his skinniness emphasized by the fact that he had not purchased any new clothes in a long time and his old ones had been bought to fit the larger frame that had formerly been his. So that his blue shirt, black pants and once-white apron seemed to hang upon him and only to touch his body where they were belted tightly at his thin waist.

His features were predominantly Mexican, the sparseness of flesh under the dark brown skin of his face accentuating the sharp angles of the bone structure. He was totally bald and seemed to ac-

6

tively compensate for this by cultivating a thick, drooping mustache, stark white in contrast to the gray bristles that sprouted for three days on his jaw and cheeks before he felt the need to shave. As far as Cuchillo was aware, Cabello never bathed.

Thus was the man's appearance in keeping with the cantina he ran—unkempt and only on nodding terms with propriety.

After completing his work in the barroom, Cuchillo went back through the archway and turned into the kitchen. Already the worst aftereffects of the drinking bout were gone and the cup of coffee he drank as he prepared and cooked a breakfast of ham, beans and grits unburdened him of all the discomforts, save for a slight thudding sensation behind his eyes.

When he took a plateful of food and cup of coffee out to Cabello, his employer continued to ignore him and began to eat, while maintaining his concentration on the English primer. Cuchillo returned to the kitchen and opened the shutters before sitting down to eat his own breakfast. The air that flowed into the small room was already hotter than that which he had breathed when looking out along Center Street. But, combined with the aroma of freshly brewed coffee it served to mask the greasy smells of old and recent cooking. And the view through the fastened back shutters was in pleasant contrast to the Apache's immediate surroundings.

He gazed into the west as he chewed and swallowed his food—down a long valley that ran between ridges of the Peloncillo Mountains toward the border between New Mexico and the Arizona Territory. Tyler Creek was at the head of the val-

7

ley, and the Mexican section of town was located close to the edge of a bluff. Thus, from any window at the rear of the cantina it was possible to get a fine panoramic view of the deep depression, which sliced arrow-straight through the jagged peaks in this part of the mountain range. And at this early morning hour, before the heat shimmer draped the terrain to move horizons closer, it was easy to imagine that a man could see almost to the distant California shore of the Pacific Ocean.

It was at the edge of the great sea that Cuchillo had last seen Captain Cyrus L. Pinner. But much further north than California, where the country had a climate that was pleasant to contemplate on the kind of searingly hot days that were the lot of southern New Mexico Territory.

On that last occasion when the horsesoldier and the Apache had come close enough to each other for their blood feud to be ended, it was the cavalry officer who had almost triumphed. And Cuchillo might have died many times since then, by the hands of White Eyes with less reason to hate him than Pinner. Up in the timber country of Oregon, or during the long trek south. But he had survived, each brush with death serving to firm his resolve to achieve his aim.

No man, though—even a singleminded Apache warrior like Cuchillo Oro—could drive himself indefinitely toward a seemingly unattainable goal without taking time out. To rest and to take stock and to plan his next move. Thus was he grateful to the town of Tyler Creek and especially appreciative of Edward Cabello's attitude toward him.

He had ridden into this White Eyes community with the brand of extreme caution experience had taught him to adopt, accepted by the Americans and Mexicans who lived there to the extent of being ignored. Which was more than any lone Indian had a right to expect in such a place. The liveryman had grunted his consent to take care of Cuchillo's horse, and the Apache had been served a drink in both the Mountain Dew Saloon and the Conquistador Cantina. Apart from the brief exchanges necessary for these transactions to be completed, nobody had spoken to the travel-weary Apache. Until Cabello had offered: "Two dollars a week and room and board, redskin. You clean up the place and you cook what we eat. Maybe you'll get to drink without payin'. Some nights I get to missin' my wife real bad, and it ain't good for a man to drink alone. Not that way. Take it or leave it. You won't get no better work in this asshole of the U.S."

It had been late at night. The rest of the town was bedded down and there were just the emaciated Cabello and the hungry Apache in the cantina. A lonely White Eyes who owned the roof over his head and a tired Indian who needed a place to stay. Cabello could not have cared less about the reception he received. Cuchillo could have survived well enough out on the desolate terrain surrounding the town. Each had known this about the other, and this knowledge had provided the cornerstone of their relationship during the following three weeks.

For a proud Apache brave, the work he had to do was demeaning—was squaw's work. But he found he was able to achieve some small degree of satisfaction from it by reaching a higher standard than Cabello demanded. This was solely for his

9

own benefit, for the skinny Mexican-American and the kind of patrons who used the Conquistador remained unaware that the cantina was cleaner than it had ever been since Señora Cabello had taken the stage for El Paso and never returned.

Cuchillo finished his breakfast and stood up with a sigh. Then he became grim-faced in earnest concentration as he moved closer to the window, peering along the valley at a tiny scatch of movement upon its broad, still floor. Already the heat of the early morning sun was generating a slick-looking shimmer in the far distance. But, just before the advancing shroud of haze veiled them, Cuchillo saw two riders heading along the trail toward Tyler Creek.

This established, he hurried to complete his morning chores. First he retrieved Cabello's plate and mug, the breakfast only a quarter eaten and the coffee hardly touched. The White Eyes ignored him. He ignored him again when, after he had washed the dishes, Cuchillo went out into the barroom again and opened the window shutters and the main door in front of the batwings.

Two old-timers—an American and a Mexican—rose arthritically from the bench outside and shuffled across the threshold.

"Mornin', Ed," the toothless American greeted. "Glad to see you're still doin' your homework."

He and the squint-eyed, round-shouldered Mexican chortled. Cabello grimaced as he slid off the high stool. He drew two glasses of warm beer and delivered them to the table by the door where the old-timers had seated themselves. Then he got his English primer and joined them, eager, but not showing it, for the day's lesson to begin.

10

Now the three men completely ignored Cuchillo as he crossed to the bead-hung archway; this was the way he liked it to be. But he was very aware of himself—for two reasons.

First there was the stink of his own body, rancid with yesterday's sweat, even more pungent in his nostrils after he had opened the door and the window shutters so that warm but fresh morning air filled the place. This was quickly dealt with in the kitchen, where he stripped naked and used water from a pan on the range to wash himself.

But there was nothing he could do about his height and his mutilated right hand—the blatantly obvious physical features, revealing, to all men who knew of the long-standing feud, that this was Pinner's Indian. He could only expect the worst and be prepared to deal with it.

Standing at the kitchen window, feeling clean and with the final effects of the hangover gone, Cuchillo watched the two riders draw near to Tyler Creek and found himself hoping they would trigger him into positive action. For his stay at the Conquistador had served its purpose. He was well-rested and had been eating better than at any other time in his life—to such an extent that his belly was starting to bulge. Not that food was entirely to blame for this, he readily admitted. One of his major faults was a liking for hard liquor and every night since his arrival at the cantina, he had been free to indulge himself in this respect. Sitting at a table out in the barroom with the skinny owner of the place, drinking steadily and not talking at all. Paying for what he had only with his attention or even mock attention. For all Cabello required of him after the last patrons had left was

11

his presence as he told and retold incidents good and bad, from his life with the woman who used to share it.

After the session on that first night, Cuchillo had learned not to interrupt the ramblings of the old man with either insincere sympathy or even simple acknowlegments. Which had allowed the Apache to think his own thoughts, his imagination running wilder the drunker her got, as his mind filled to overflowing with vicious schemes to extract revenge from the hated Pinner.

Then Edward Cabello would pass out and Cuchillo would lift him from the chair and take him to his room, and he would go to his own sleeping quarters, to experience the initial process of sobering up as he lay awake for a few mintues. The thousand mental images of Pinner suffering excruciating death agonies would fade and the Apache would begin to suffer himself. Shame that he accepted the humiliation of working for Cabello for such self-indulgent reasons. Bitterness that there was scant hope of getting a line on the whereabouts of Pinner while he remained in Tyler Creek, becoming bloated with food and liquor. Self-disgust that he had got drunk of his own volition, fully aware of the unpleasant symptoms he would experience when he awoke the next morning.

Now, as he watched the two riders out of sight—the stagecoach trail took them to the right, went around the bluff and made the final approach to town up the northern slope—he shook his mind free of its uncharacteristically wishful thoughts. And vented a low, but powerful curse in his native

12

tongue as he once more experienced shame, bitterness and self-disgust.

The two newcomers to Tyler Creek might or might not come to the Conquistador Cantina. They might or might not see him. They might or might not see he was exceptionally tall for an Apache and had a crippled right hand. Might or might not have heard about Pinner's Indian. Might or might not be aware that the cavalry captain had posted a four-hundred-dollar reward for the golden knife and a thousand-dollar bounty for Cuchillo Oro alive.

Whatever they did or did not know about him, it made no difference to Cuchillo in terms of his ultimate goal. Which should have been his attitude when he first arrived in Tyler Creek and on each occasion when he had watched other strangers ride in on horseback or aboard the stage. For the Apache was his own man, free of all constraints for as long as he kept his wits about him, capable of following whatever action he chose.

"You dumb Mescalero," he muttered forcefully to himself in English as he turned away from the window. And then he grinned foolishly—and affectionately—as a fleeting memory of John Hedges flitted across his mind. His old teacher at the Borderline Rancheria, and one of the few White Eyes he called a friend. With the exception of the heavy drinking each night, John Hedges would have been very pleased to hear about the attitude his star pupil had adopted during the stay in Tyler Creek. Then the smile was wiped from the dark, strong lines of Cuchillo's face. "It is only old men who should sit and wait for death."

"Hey, redskin!" Cabello yelled from the barroom.

"Breakfast for one! And hurry it up, you lazy son of a no-good squaw!"

Cuchillo reacted automatically to the order, crossing to the stove, adding more fuel to the flames and tipping fat into the skillet. Which left his mind free to work along independent lines.

And allowed him to postpone the decision about precisely what course of action he should adopt to leave Tyler Creek and find Cyrus L. Pinner.

The customer who wanted breakfast was a stranger in town. All the regular patrons of the cantina were aware that an Apache was employed there, and Cabello no longer had to make his feelings toward Cuchillo so cruelly clear with his bad mouth. Only when a newcomer entered did he snarl such insults.

So, forcing his true feelings deep down inside himself, the Apache cooked the meal the best way he knew how and carried it on a tray out of the kitchen, along the hallway and into the barroom. As he pushed through the bead curtain, the features of his handsome face were set impassively and his dark eyes appeared to show total disinterest as he surveyed the new customer seated at a table close to the bar.

The man was an American. About forty. Tall and broadly built with closely cropped black hair above an ugly, pockmarked face. He was dressed in a black shirt, black pants, black riding boots with rusted spurs, and a black Stetson, which hung down his back on the lanyard. He wore a gunbelt with the holster on the left, the Remington revolver positioned for a cross draw. He was dusty from a long trip and his blue eyes were red-rimmed and heavily bagged from lack of sleep.

14

The eyes looked at Cuchillo as if the Apache was something slimy, which had crawled out from under a rock. The thin lips curled back to show discolored teeth in a sneer of contempt. But there was nothing in the expression that came close to recognition. The man looked toward the anxious Edward Cabello, who was behind the bar now, and the scorn remained firmly set on his features.

"I guess I'm hungry enough to eat buzzard so long as it was plucked, mister," he growled, and shifted his hard-eyed gaze to Cuchillo as the Apache set down the tray in front of him. "But I tell you . . . if my guts didn't figure my throat was cut, I'd kick your ass from one end of this stinkin' town to the other. For just lettin' an injun be in the same room where my food was bein' cooked."

"Señor," Cabello blurted with a broad, sick grin, the expression and his voice playing up the Mexican side of his heritage. "This redskin, he cooks like a dream, believe me."

"Dreams I get for nothin' when I lay my head down, mister. Right now it's my butt that's down. In a chair at a table. An' if this grub costs me money, it'd better be damn good."

He continued to glower at Cuchillo as he augmented his threat to Cabello. Then he started to eat as the Apache moved away, back toward the bead-hung archway.

"I tasted worse," the newcomer allowed by way of a verdict after he had shoveled three mouthfuls of food between his lips.

Cabello sighed his relief and drew two more beers in payment for a further lesson from the toothless old-timer.

Cuchillo withdrew behind the beads and returned to the kitchen, having to quell anger now. Not directed at the cowering Edward Cabello, or even the tough talking, Indian-hating stranger. For he knew well and had grown used to the skinny owner of the cantina and his ways. And he was familiar from long experience with the type of man who was eating breakfast. Instead, his fury was turned inward at himself for continuing to leave himself open to such humiliating treatment, and for no other reason than that he was waiting for an outside influence to spur him into moving on.

For what seemed a long time he sat at the table in the kitchen, gazing out through the window at the mountain vista against which nothing moved anymore. Somehow the long, broad valley honed a sharper edge to his bitterness. It was old Apache land—wild and empty and free—where a skilled brave wise in the ways of his nation could live adequately, if not as comfortably as in a White Eyes town. Yet the valley and the equally wild and empty and free terrain, which stretched out in every other direction from Tyler Creek, comprised an encircling trap. For which direction should he take? Which expanse of empty country should he cover to pick up the trail of the hated Pinner?

At the start, the Southwest had been Pinner's domain. Then he had showed up in San Francisco, but that had been on personal business, or perhaps some special assignment. After his failure on the cold and savage sea of the north, had Pinner returned to the Southwest? By choice or by dictate of higher military authority, he could have left the dust and heat of Arizona and New Mexico Territories forever. At this moment he might be a thousand or two thousand miles away. In which direction?

Footfalls sounded in the hallway and Cuchillo rose to his feet as the stranger with the pock-marked face appeared at the doorway, his empty plate and coffee mug in his hands. The food seemed to have mellowed him a little, or perhaps it was just that weariness had taken some of the hardness out of his eyes. His discolored teeth continued to be bared in a scowl.

"You cook real good, injun," he growled. "Same again for me. And two more likewise for a couple of my old buddies that are comin' down the street." He advanced into the kitchen and set the dirty dishes and cutlery down on the table. He was at least three inches shorter than the towering height of the Apache and he backed away hurriedly, as if this difference made him uncomfortable—even nervous. "Hell, you're big for an injun, ain't you?" he rasped.

For a brief moment, Cuchillo experienced a flush of pride, but not because of the accident of his stature. Rather because his build was inherited— once removed—from a great chief of the Mimbrenos Apaches. For he was the grandson of Mangas Coloradas, who also stood tall, higher from the ground even than Cuchillo.

Then the pride was gone, to be replaced by a powerful shame. His grandfather had, indeed, been a great chief in more ways than one. But what would that fine old man think of his grandson could he see him now—doing squaw's work for the White Eyes without even the excuse of duress? Surely Mangas would disown him, and therefore it was empty vanity to feel pride at their relationship.

17

"To look at," Cuchillo said softly as he turned to the range, putting his broad back to the American. "But sometimes the tallest of trees may be hollow."

The man in the doorway grunted his confusion, then said, "You lost me, injun."

His footfalls sounded in the hallway again as he headed back to the barroom.

"I think maybe I lost myself," the Apache said miserably as he listened to the hot fat sizzling in the skillet.

CHAPTER TWO

The two men who joined the one with the pock-marked face at the table by the bar were the riders Cuchillo had seen approach Tyler Creek along the valley from the west. He recognized them from their clothes—all black in the manner of the first stranger to enter the Conquistador. Both of them were about ten years younger. One was a blond and the other had red hair. In addition to the revolvers in their holsters, each carried a Sharps rifle into the cantina, which he rested against the edge of the table.

It was obvious they had been warned an Apache was to cook and serve their meal for they eyed Cuchillo with nothing more than idle curiosity when he emerged from the archway, and tasted the food without interest. Only by spooning more into their mouths did they pass an opinion on what it was like. They were less travel-stained than the older man and had slept and shaved recently.

"You ever seen an injun that big, Polk?" the pockmarked man asked.

The blond-haired man glanced indifferently across the barroom and shrugged his broad shoulders. "Tell you the truth, Farley, I see one or even two injuns I don't hardly notice 'em. Anymore than

19

that, I don't stick around long enough to look close."

"You're right, he cooks good," the red-headed man put in. "You hear anythin' from Hewitt yet?"

Cuchillo withdrew to the kitchen. Preferring the view of the valley to the street scene outside the window of his room. He kept his mind clear now, not marking the passage of time with futile thoughts. And the day ran its blisteringly hot course almost as uneventfully as all the others since he had reached town. Customers came and went in the barroom, all of them regular patrons. Three ordered lunch and Cuchillo cooked and served the meals, the ingredients the same as at breakfast. For the rest, only drinks were required and Cabello supplied these.

The presence of the three strangers provided the only break with routine, and they were something of a topic of conversation with the predominantly Mexican regular customers—on two counts. Firstly, they were Americans and as such it seemed odd they should choose to drink at the cantina instead of the Mountain Dew Saloon at the eastern end of Center Street. Secondly, there was their huge capacity for drink. Rye for the two younger men and beer for Farley.

They left the table only to go to the latrine out back of the place and, after the first fifteen minutes, they spoke only to order more drinks from Cabello.

Initially, the skinny owner of the Conquistador had been anxious about the heavy drinking of the trio. So much so that he had come out into the kitchen to tell Cuchillo to run down the street to the law office the moment trouble started. But, as morning gave way to afternoon, which in turn surrendered to the advance of evening, his fears appeared to be groundless.

The strangers seemed to be untouched by the alcohol. They simply sat and drank and gazed into space: apparently locked into a private world of their own making, emerging only when their glasses were empty or their bladders full.

During the course of the day the word was spread about them and local citizens came to the Conquistador to look at them and whisper about them. But, if they were aware of being a center of interest, the trio chose to ignore it.

When night had fully descended upon the town, Polk called for a meal and the other two told Cabello that they would eat as well.

"It will be the same as breakfast, señors," Cabello apologized nervously.

"Guess we're near as hungry as we was then, mister," Farley answered. "So just put the injun to work, huh."

"Si, señor."

The skinny old man did not shout the order. Instead, he went again to the kitchen, where Cuchillo sat in the dark, peering out at the moonlit valley. At night the terrain looked even emptier, wilder and freer than in daylight. Thus was its call toward his Apache mind and heart much stronger.

"Three more meals for the strangers," Cabello instructed as he struck a match to light a coal-oil lamp. "And you can bed down after you done that, I figure. The one with the pitted face, I don't think he'd like to have you drinkin' in the same place he is. And he pays, redskin."

Cuchillo showed no response and Cabello returned to the barroom, a greedy glint in his eyes. The Apache closed the shutters against the swarm of moths that tried to zoom in toward the light. During the quiet afternoon his sole chore had been to keep the fire from dying. Thus, all he had to do now was add more fuel to the flames in order to ready the skillet for the food.

"Wait right there, injun," Farley ordered after Cuchillo had set down the three plates of steaming food at the table by the bar.

The Conquistador was doing the same kind of business it usually did at this time of night and the Apache recognized by sight the ten Mexicans and one American who were drinking at tables or standing at the bar. These regular customers had now become used to the presence of the trio of taciturn strangers and were ignoring them. And, as was usual, no one paid any attention to Cuchillo as he moved among the tables.

Until the man with the pockmarked face issued the soft-spoken, slightly slurred command. The hum of conversation was abruptly curtained, and for stretched seconds the silence would have been total had it not been for the pattering sounds of moths and flying insects attempting suicide against the glass funnels of three coal-oil lamps. In that time every pair of eyes swung toward the table by the bar and began to flick between the faces of Farley and Cuchillo. The sweat beads that stood out on every brow seemed to glisten more brightly in the dim light, which coned down from the ceiling-hung lamps.

"Somethin' is wrong with the food, señor?" Cabello asked anxiously, standing up from the stool, which was now behind the bar.

"Looks fine to me, Farley," the man with red hair muttered, and started to fork grits into his mouth.

"How's it taste, Brookes?"

"Fine." He shrugged as he gave the reply.

Farley showed his heavily stained teeth in a drunken grin. His attention swung away from Brookes and he looked up at the impassive face of Cuchillo. "Never really thought it'd be anythin' else, injun." There was a spare chair at the table and he scraped it across the floor with a foot. "Sit down. Bartender, a drink for the chef!"

He laughed and it was an ugly sound.

Cuchillo saw Polk and Brookes stiffen, then bend their heads over their plates to continue eating when Farley winked. A burst of talk was loud in the cantina, its tone angry.

"Cabello!" the skinny man's elderly English teacher snapped. "We don't mind you got an Apache workin' at your place. But we ain't gonna sit in the same room drinkin' with one of his kind."

The American's words cut across the many exchanges and drew emphatic nods of agreement from those who had been interrupted.

Cabello's nervousness expanded and a tic began to twitch the flaccid skin beneath his right eye.

Farley's expression and voice suddenly became hard as he addressed the skinny man, his gaze sweeping across the angry faces of the other patrons. "Like for the injun to join me and my buddies," he insisted. "Reckon we spent a lot of money in this asshole of a place today. Only thing that'd stop us spending a lot more is if we couldn't get what we wanted. Seems to me, bartender, that the customer oughta always be right. But you got

23

yourself a problem. Which customer? The one that spends big? Or the one that puts out a couple of pesos, then only spends time nursing the one lousy beer he's bought?"

This said, Farley began to eat, washing down each mouthful of food with a swig of beer.

Cuchillo was left to stand at the table beside the offered chair, while Cabello scowled at his dilemma in face of his angry regular customers. Once again Cuchillo was a pawn in a dangerous game controlled by White Eyes, and tormented by anger for allowing himself to be maneuvered into another humiliating situation.

Then Cabello vented a low Spanish curse and reached a shot glass and a bottle of rye off a shelf. The elderly American was the first to rise and turn toward the batwings.

"You guys disgust me!" the cantina owner snarled, having to work hard to get the right note into his anger. "I gave the redskin work out of the goodness of my heart! He's a man, like any other! Except that he's of a different race!"

Men turned away from the bar to follow others toward the clean, fresh night that lay on the other side of the batwings, beyond the fetid atmosphere trapped in the room. No one looked back at the skinny man as he began to shout the truth mixed in with other lies.

"I'll tell you mean bastards a secret! Every night after you leave this place, me and the redskin been drinkin' together! Here in this room! It didn't never bother me, on account of I ain't got nothin' against him just because he's an Apache!"

The sound of boots on the floor and the dry creaking of the batwings seemed to be amplified

24

by the verbal silence of the men who were walking out of the Conquistador. The tic worked faster on the sparse flesh of Cabello's face and his voice rose to a higher pitch.

"I tell you somethin' else!" he shrieked. "You walk outta my place like this, you won't never come back in again!" The last man stepped out over the threshold and the doors swung a final time and were still. Cabello was silent for a moment while he brought himself under control. Abruptly he was pale-faced and looked on the verge of keeling over.

"You wanna bring that bottle over here now?" Farley asked. "And another glass as well. Figure I'll switch to hard liquor. Get some real drinkin' done."

He waved a hand, which ordered the Apache to sit on the chair, and Cuchillo complied without hesitation. For there had been plenty of time for him to assess his position during the mass walkout and Cabello's near-hysterical reaction to it. There was going to be trouble, that was certain. All the men were bored and had failed to relieve their feelings with alcohol. Polk and Brookes could handle the slow passage of time, but Farley had run out of patience. So it was the eldest of the trio who would instigate whatever new brand of evil was to enter the life of Cuchillo Oro—who had already decided there was just one slim hope for himself. To play the game the White Eyes wanted for as long as he could steel himself against the urge to retaliate. What happened then was in the hands of the Great Spirits.

"So the injun's got a taste for liquor, has he?" Farley asked Cabello as the skinny man placed the bottle and two glasses on the table among the almost-empty plates.

"Sure has," Cabello answered dully, shifting his eyes away from the batwings to glare malevolently at the Apache. "He drinks it like most men drink water."

All three Americans finished eating and rattled their cutlery down on the plates.

"Get rid of what we don't want no more," Farley told Cabello, fisting a hand around the neck of the uncorked bottle and tilting it over the two empty glasses.

Still directing his anger at Cuchillo, electing to blame him for all that had happened and was about to happen, Cabello collected the soiled plates.

"Do anythin' interestin' when he's loaded?" Farley asked as he pushed one of the brimful glasses toward Cuchillo, who responded to the White Eyes' cruel grin with a look of cool composure.

Cabello had started to take the dirty crocks toward the beaded archway. Now he set them down on a convenient table and went to the bar, his anger replaced by anxiety. He tried to hide this behind a grin.

"The redskin is a good listener, señor. My wife, she left me and it brought me great sadness. I would be drunk all the time if I did not have this business to run. But I drink only at the most lonely time. Which is at night. The redskin, he drinks with me. And he listens when I talk about Maria. But I think maybe I get drunk before he does. And I do not see what he—"

Farley waved a hand to silence Cabello, then withdrew the glass from in front of the Apache and

26

pushed the bottle forward. His grin broadened and expressed greater evil, then was abruptly wiped from his face as he rasped, "Drink up, injun. If it takes a long time, we don't wanna waste any while we keep pourin' you shots."

Polk had lit a cheroot and was picking at his teeth with the end of the dead match. Brookes, who was directly across the table from Cuchillo, looked unhappy with what was going on. Farley saw this and snarled, "You're a miserable bastard, Harry! On account of there ain't nothin' to entertain a man in this lousy town. No dance hall. No whores. Not even any gamblin'. So I fix up some entertainment for us and still you look like you got a gutache and an earache at the same time."

The red-haired man grimaced. "Just thinkin' that Hewitt wouldn't like us to start no trouble, is all."

"He's right," Polk added, although his expression as he continued to dig between his teeth suggested his mind was still on other things.

"Trouble?" Farley asked with a look of mock innocence. "Who's startin' trouble? Just inviting the injun to drink with us, is all. Give him a chance to let his hair down. His kind don't get a lot of fun out of life, I reckon." The grin had reappeared as he spoke. Now it was wiped off his pitted face as he swung toward Cuchillo. "I told you to drink up!" he forced from between compressed lips.

The two younger men showed their acceptance of the situation by withdrawing into private worlds of their own thinking: Polk busy with his teeth picking chore, and Brookes staring down into his near-empty glass as he rolled it between both palms. They had tried to influence Farley and had failed.

Behind the bar, Cabello hoisted himself back on

to his stool and hunched over the schoolbook. But his attitude of concentration was obviously faked because he constantly raised his chin up from his cupped palms to glance fearfully toward the table.

For a few more stretched seconds in the sweating, rancid-smelling silence, Cuchillo Oro remained as inwardly placid as he seemed on the surface. But then the short leash on his anger snapped, the strain placed upon it compounded as much by the indifference of Polk and Brookes and the cringing fear of Cabello as by the overt cruelty of Farley.

He picked up the rye bottle with his good left hand fisted around the neck. And channeled the full extent of his emotions toward Farley as the pockmarked face became spread with an ugly grin of triumph.

"That's it, injun," Farley rasped. "Do like a white man tells you. Drink up and then show us a dance. The kind that clap-raddled squaws do. On account you're doin' squaw's work in this lousy can—"

Cuchillo had the bottle halfway from the table to his lips, his mind closed to what Farley was saying. For further insults were meaningless. Just as a man can be made to suffer to a degree of agony beyond which his capacity to feel physical pain is exhausted, so had Cuchillo's pride as an Apache brave been attacked too often. This baiting by a drunken stranger finally tripped the scales, which had been drastically overweighted on the wrong side during his stay at the Conquistador.

The bottle was in his left hand and Farley sat diagonally across from him on that side. For a vital second he was able to remain outwardly composed, earning him another fragment of time from the advantage of shock.

His left hand descended—much faster than he had raised it, and on a slightly different arc. His wrist was turned just enough to cause the side of the bottle to crash against the edge of the table.

The glass shattered and strong-smelling whiskey flooded across the table top and splashed to the floor.

Cabello straightened fast and forcefully on his stool, and shrieked in alarm as he tipped backward, rattling bottles and glasses on the shelves behind him.

Polk and Brookes grunted as they were jerked out of their reveries into the dangerous reality of the present; their day-long drinking session had slowed their responses to the threat.

Farley's mind was also besotted by alcohol and his reflexes were hampered by naked fear of violent death. For the part of the bottle still gripped by the Apache was raised and then swung forward in a stabbing action, the jagged circle of glinting broken glass aimed directly toward his face. His first instinctive action was to protect his eyes and he brought his hands up while terror continued to hold him fast in the chair.

Cuchillo was already on his feet and leaning forward by then, his chair sent tipping backward by the force of his lunge.

"Dear sweet Jesus!" Farley rasped—and only now pressed his feet hard against the floor to power himself backward. Which exposed his belly and the Remington in the cross-drawn holster on the left.

Even as he hooked the revolver out of the holster with the thumb of his crippled hand, the Apache found a fragment of time in which to hate Pinner for causing the terrible injury. Then to feel relief that the three Americans had spent the whole day drinking.

For he had allowed himself to be outnumbered against men with superior weapons, and then had recklessly started an offensive that should have been doomed to fatal failure.

But the Great Spirits smiled on him, compensating in some small degree for all the bad fortune they had showered upon him.

Farley continued to fall backward in his chair until it crashed to the floor and tipped him out. Polk and Brookes were driven by haste into time-wasting clumsiness as they went for their holstered revolvers and powered upright.

Cuchillo was standing at his full height by then, the top section of the broken bottle falling to the floor as he snatched the Remington with his good hand, cocked the hammer and angled the barrel down at Farley.

"I no wish to kill!" he shouted, louder than was necessary but anxious for his intentions to register in the liquor-addled brains of the two younger men.

"Hold it, you guys!" Farley cried, absolutely motionless on the floor beside the overturned chair as he looked up at the muzzle of his own Remington aimed down at him. As he spoke he managed to tear his gaze away from the gun and swivel his eyes to the full extent of the sockets, to back his words with a look of desperate pleading.

Polk and Brookes—as pale as Cabello, who peered over the top of the bar—had their guns drawn and cocked, and were just on the point of swinging them to aim at the Apache.

"But Boyd—" Polk started.

"He's got me, goddamnit!" Farley snarled.

"Put guns on table and back away," Cuchillo commanded. "I will not kill . . . unless I have to."

Cabello straightened up behind the bar. "Do it, señors," he urged as the tic began to work frantically across his cheek again. Then his eyes were filled with the same kind of plea Farley was expressing. "They was just funnin', redskin," he blurted. "You shouldn't have took it so serious. Ain't that right?"

Farley tried to speak, but only made a croaking sound. He nodded vigorously. Polk and Brookes began to slide the guns back into their holsters, but their gazes remained fixed upon the Apache's face.

"Give him back his gun and let's forget the whole thing," Cabello hurried on. "The town don't like having my place here. Any trouble and I'll be closed up for sure. I been good to you, ain't I, redskin?"

There had been a brief moment as he thought about Pinner when the proudly handsome face of Cuchillo had been contorted into a scowl of cruel viciousness. But now his features were composed again, masking his contempt for the skinny man's plea. His tone was just as unrevealing, the words he spoke sufficient in themselves as he raised his mutilated hand.

"It is good that only one hand suffered this punishment instead of two, White Eyes. That is how good you have been to me."

Then he squeezed the trigger of the Remington and four men gasped. But Farley was unhurt, the

31

bullet drilling into the floor an inch away from the head of the man with the pitted face, kicking up sawdust into his eyes.

"What the hell?" Polk snarled as he and Brookes froze in the act of reaching for their guns.

"I said to put revolvers on the table," Cuchillo reminded. "Not in holsters. You not do that now, I kill him. Maybe you, and you also. Before I die."

"Shit!" Cabello groaned, deep in a slough of misery. "There ain't never been a shot fired in my place. Carson's sure to close me down—"

"Do like he says!" Farley pleaded, his pores pumping out enough of the sweat of terror to wash the sawdust off his cheekbones and down into his stubble.

His two partners complied, lifting their Navy Colts from the holsters with nervous delicacy, each holding the butt between a thumb and forefinger, and then lowering the guns gently onto the table top. They backed away until they came up against the bar front.

The Apache nodded his satisfaction and began to move backward himself, toward the batwings. He swung the Remington from left to right, threatening each of the men in turn. Farley decided it was safe to ease up into a sitting posture. A bone in his arm cracked. It was the only sound louder than the thud of flying creatures hitting the lamps. For everyone in the cantina was holding his breath, and Cuchillo's moccasined feet were silent as he lowered them to the floor.

He smelled the familiar scents of the Conquistador—the spilled liquor, the tobacco smoke, the cooking grease and the sweat of his own and other bodies. And his spirits rose at the prospect of leaving such acrid taints, and all they meant, behind him. The vista he had seen so often from the kitchen window—of the broad valley and jagged ridges—had never been so appealing. He could almost feel grateful to the three strangers in Tyler Creek for forcing him to leave.

Then, as the mountain night put an edge of coolness on the air that flowed into the cantina over and under the batwings, he sensed danger. And he silently cursed himself at giving in to the impulse to explode a shot at the floor.

The silence inside the Conquistador should not have been matched outside. Tyler Creek was a quiet, law-abiding town in which only Sheriff John Carson regularly carried a gun. A gunshot in the night should have caused shock and aroused curiosity.

A man behind Cuchillo expelled his pent-up breath as the Apache took the backward step that began to push open the batwing doors.

Something made a swishing sound through the air.

The lines of misery deepened in the skin of Cabello's face.

Grins of evil delight spread across the faces of the three disarmed gunmen.

Cuchillo was hit hard on the side of his head, just above his right ear. His mind filled with a mental image of the mountainscape to the west of Tyler Creek. The sun raced across the blue sky and changed color from yellow to crimson while it was still many hours away from the distant horizon. Then the great red orb exploded and showered flames of agonizing fire downward.

Night came suddenly. To shroud everything. Even pain.

Somebody asked: "How you feeling?"

From out of the pitch darkness, abruptly filled with fresh waves of pain, the Apache replied, "Like I wish I had none."

CHAPTER THREE

"What was that?"

Cuchillo's groaning response to the first inquiry had sounded deafeningly loud to his own ears. The second question angered him and he snapped open his eyes to see who was tormenting him. The pain in his head did not get worse but bright sunlight irritated his eyes. So he half closed them and it was easier to look out between the bars of his eyelashes—toward thicker, stronger bars of steel that formed one wall of the cell in the Tyler Creek jailhouse.

He had never been there before, but he knew exactly where he was because he recognized the man who was peering in at him through the bars.

Sheriff John Carson, who was neither the best nor the worst White Eyes the Apache had ever met.

"You figure you need a doctor to take a look at you?" the lawman asked, dutifully rather than anxiously.

Cuchillo was lying on a cot comprised of a single blanket draped over a raised plank. When he sat up and swung his feet to the cement floor his spine protested almost as forcefully as his head. His response to the new agony was a grunt, which interrupted his thought processes as he recalled the events that had led to him being in the cell. His recollections completed, he added the fact of the strong sunlight and asked: "How long?"

"I can get Doc Adams over here in five minutes," Carson answered.

Cuchillo shook his head and regretted it. "I mean how long have I been here?"

Carson consulted a large watch, which he drew from a vest pocket on a chain. "Seven A.M. now, Indian. Laid my gun butt across your skull at ten last night." He put the watch away. "That's a long time for a man to be unconscious. Reason I asked if you needed a doctor."

"No. I have hard head, lawman."

Carson grimaced. "Maybe your skull is. But what's underneath must be mush, I reckon. For you to tangle with those gunslingers at the cantina."

The sheriff of Tyler Creek was a distinguished-looking man nearing the far end of middle age and making efforts to grow old gracefully. He was tall and slim, with just a suggestion of thickening around the waist. He had always been handsome and he had the kind of clear, evenly tanned skin stretched over well-formed features that improved with maturity. His hair was silver with just a strand here and there of the original black. His eyes were blue and clear, and his teeth were white and even. He dressed like a city dude, except for the workaday gunbelt with its holstered Navy Colt slung around his waist. And, although he was never seen in public without a crisp white shirt and newly pressed vest, he never wore the matching jacket to his pants unless in church on Sundays.

"You are not concerned that they began the trouble, lawman?" Cuchillo asked, getting tentatively to his feet. He swayed just a little.

"They said you drank too much and started insulting whites," Carson answered. "Cabello backed their story, but I didn't pay too much mind to that. That man would always side with the strongest side—principles and rights having nothing to do with it." He shrugged. "But it don't matter."

"To who?" the Apache asked, going to the barred window and peering out at the morning.

"Everybody but you, I guess. One of those gunslingers wanted your hide nailed to the front of the courthouse. But the others made him see sense. All three of them plan on leaving Tyler Creek today. After they meet up with a buddy scheduled to ride in. Soon as they've gone, I'll turn you loose. Cabello doesn't reckon to press charges. Just told me to warn you not to try to go back to the Conquistador."

"Like life," Cuchillo muttered.

"What?"

"I brought nothing in, lawman. There is nothing for me to take out."

"He pay you?" Carson asked.

"Not yet. I will need money if I am to get horse from livery stable."

The sheriff grunted as he turned away from the bars. "I'll see you get what's owed you. Yell out when you're ready to eat."

His footsteps scraped on the cement floor and then he closed the door, which blocked off his office from the hallway and opened onto the three

37

cells of the jailhouse block. The total silence that closed in after this made it plain Cuchillo was the only prisoner in custody.

Left alone with his pain and bitterness, the Apache spared a few moments to feel gratitude toward Sheriff Carson, who had done for him more than he expected of most White Eyes. Many others, whether lawmen or not, would have either shot him down out of hand, or used the slender pretext of the scene at the Conquistador to summarily lynch the Indian.

Then the depressing view from the cell window acted to drive such reasoned thoughts about the attitudes of a near stranger out of Cuchillo's mind.

The law office and cell block was on the northern side of Center Street, about midway between the cantina and the Mountain Dew Saloon, which faced each other along the length of the street. The windows—frosted in the office and barred in the cells—looked out on the street. A broad street flanked by well-constructed buildings at the eastern, American end, and crudely built ones in the Mexican quarter of town. Brick, stone and timber. Or adobe.

Even if he had not overheard talk in the cantina, Cuchillo would have recognized from the size and design of Tyler Creek that it had once been a proud, forward-looking town established by people with high hopes for the future. The reason for establishing a community at the head of the long valley had been silver. Enough had been found in the surrounding mountains for the prospectors' tent town to be replaced by something more substantial. Then a mining company cooperative had been set up and the Americans who financed this became rich enough to hire Mexican labor. Thus had Tyler Creek spread westward and eastward from its original nucleus, and at that time there had been between the American and Mexican sections, a clear line of demarcation, which was as well-established socially as it seemed to be from the two distinct styles of architecture.

But then the silver ran out and Tyler Creek went into a steep decline. It might have become just one more ghost town of the Southwestern territories had it not been for the staunch reluctance of a handful of the old prospectors to believe the ore-bearing rock was exhausted. Many moved away, but these few remained—and, because of the smallness of their number, they had survived. For, every now and then, a minor strike was made, sufficient to keep the town in existence, even though as a tarnished semblance of what it once had been.

To the north and south of Center Street, the cross streets were lined with buildings, which were for the most part empty and derelict. While on the town's main thoroughfare an attempt had been made to keep up appearances. It had failed.

Immediately across from where Cuchillo Oro peered out at the new day, through eyes in danger of becoming blurred with pain, was the Tyler Creek People's Bank. The only two-story building in town. To one side of it was the stage depot, and on the other the church. Because of the thickness of the jailhouse walls, he could see no further. But he knew, from the many times he had looked out of the window of his room at the cantina, what the rest of Center Street was like.

To the west of his vantage point was the courthouse; to the east the livery stable. Elsewhere along the street in both directions were houses and stores, erected initially to cater exclusively to either Americans or Mexicans. Now some of these buildings were empty and all were as badly neglected as the bank, stage depot and church Cuchillo could see. For what silver did come out of the surrounding hills was sufficient only to pay for the necessities of life. Such items as paint for weather protection, new glass for broken windows, and fresh timber to replace that which was warped or rotted were luxuries.

With the exception of the debonair Sheriff John Carson, the citizens of Tyler Creek were a match for their town: used up, weary of life, lacking hope for the future, and too disenchanted to work harder than necessary. Dissatisfied with their lot, but unprepared to make any effort to improve it.

He watched many of them now, commencing their daily routine in the rising heat of the New Mexico morning. Miners setting off for the surrounding country. Merchants opening up their premises for the day. Women starting their shopping. Children heading for the schoolhouse. Americans mingling with Mexicans, separated by style of clothing and facial characteristics, but united by weariness and depression.

Such people might have accepted an Apache among them out of a sense of empathy for an individual as ill-treated as they were by life. But Cuchillo had never believed this to be true. The citizens of Tyler Creek were simply too dispirited to experience strong emotions of any kind.

And Sheriff Carson, despite his strenuous efforts to keep up appearances, was very much one with the people it was his duty to protect. He did the least that was expected of him, which explained why he had been content to deal with Cuchillo by smacking him over the head with a gun butt and tossing him in jail.

As he stood by the cell window, allowing time to crawl into dull history, the pain in his head subsided to a nagging ache. Became bearable to such an extent that, as he heard the approach of the morning stage along the cross street from the western trail, he was able to form his features into a wry grin. For, he had suddenly realized, he had allowed himself to be infected by the malady of Tyler Creek during his stay in the town.

Had he not been as apathetic as everyone else while he endured the demeaning work at the Conquistador? Failed to be moved to a positive response by anything until the White Eyes named Farley had forced him to act?

The grin expanded to a short laugh as the stage turned onto Center Street and came to a smooth halt in front of the depot. At the same time, the door from the law office opened and keys on a ring jangled against each other.

He turned at the sound of one of the keys being slid into the lock of the cell door.

"I'm happy you're happy," Carson drawled flatly. "And you ought to be, considering the amount of luck you have for a lone Apache."

He swung the door open and tossed a ball of paper onto the cot. Cuchillo saw that the ball was comprised of some dollar bills screwed up tight.

"Cabello paid?" He was surprised.

"Told you I'd get it," the lawman replied. "And I always keep my word. So you can leave. Seems the three strangers left town in the middle of the night without waiting for their buddy to show up."

"Me?"

"Leave town or stay. If you stay, don't cause any trouble."

He shrugged and turned away from the open door. Cuchillo was about to follow him, pausing only to pick up the ball of bills from the cot. But then, on the periphery of his vision, he glimpsed the figure of a man clad in a familiar garb.

He swung his head slowly, to look again out of the barred window and across the dusty, sun-bright street toward the stagecoach parked outside the depot.

Several local citizens were gathered around the stage, generating an aura of subdued excitement, and for a moment the Apache thought he must have been mistaken. He chided himself for being tricked by an imagination feeding on impossible, wishful thoughts. But then, as a woman emerged from the open offside door of the stage and the feelings of the watchers became more vocal, his interest heightened again. There was a stir of movement and, because his full attention was now concentrated upon the street, he knew there had been no mistake.

Through a gap in the throng he saw that the man who was helping the woman to climb down from the stage was dressed in U.S. Army blue.

Despite his attempts to quell his emotions, Cuchillo was unable to check a grunt of evil anticipation. Which, a split second later, became an animalistic snarl as a further movement among the crowd offered him a clear view of the soldier. He recognized the gold braid insignia of a cavalry captain, but the officer had his back to the street as he used both hands to steady the woman's final step down from the stage.

His height was right, though.

So was his build.

Cuchillo screwed his eyes closed tight and compressed his lips over teeth set in a snarl. His head suddenly hurt worse than ever, as did his back, and he reached a hand around and under his shirt. He sighed when his fingers closed on the handle of the golden knife.

Then he opened his eyes as the gathering across the street gave vent to a full-throated cheer of wild enthusiasm, surging in on the new arrivals—but not before Cuchillo saw the beaming faces of the woman and the man.

The captain was in his early thirties, two inches above six feet and well-built. He had a handsome, sun-bronzed face under short-trimmed, heavily greased black hair. His eyes were green, and though he was showing his white, very even teeth, there was an unmistakable twist of cruelty in the set of his lips. The way he held his head atop the short neck gave him a look of arrogance.

The welcoming crowd jostled to kiss the cheeks of the woman and to pump the hand of the man. But nobody in Tyler Creek experienced a greater happiness than Cuchillo Oro at seeing Captain Cyrus L. Pinner.

Then the man the Apache had vowed to kill was abruptly weary of the attentions of the welcoming crowd and he glanced with distaste along Center Street. As his green eyes raked across the jailhouse facade, Cuchillo drew hurriedly back from the bars.

For part of a second, until the final remnants of shock had left him, his mind did not function properly and he thought he was still a prisoner—trapped in a cell and helplessly at the mercy of his cruel enemy. But then he saw the ball of dollar bills on the cot and the half-open door.

He licked the salt beads of tension sweat off his upper lip, snatched up the money, and took long strides out into the hallway.

Carson kept his office as neat and clean as his appearance. It held a desk, two chairs, a safe, two cabinets and a rifle rack. The door to the street was open and the sheriff stood on the threshold, leaning a shoulder against the jamb as he surveyed the activity in front of the stage depot. He heard the Apache enter the office behind him and glanced disinterestedly over his shoulder.

"Return of local girl who made good in the big city," he drawled. "Reckon there'll be a big celebration—"

A burst of gunfire counterpointed by the shattering of glass curtailed the lawman's dully spoken sentence. And he raked his attention back to the street as screams and lower-pitched cries of alarm ended a moment of stunned silence.

"Jesus, the bank!" Carson gasped incredulously and lunged out of the doorway, clawing the Colt from the holster.

Cuchillo remained where he was for perhaps two seconds, receiving a wide-angle view of the street through the big window of the law office.

The people were no longer in a close-knit group at the side of the stage, but instead were racing across and along the street in search of cover as far away from the front of the bank as possible.

The bank had a solid wood door with frosted glass windows to either side. Both these windows were broken now and a man was folded double over the sill of one of them, blood dripping slowly from out of his lank hair to stain the dirt street.

Another burst of gunfire exploded as Cuchillo strode to Carson's desk and scooped up the bunch of keys that lay there. The bullets cracked out through the smashed windows of the bank and one of the running men came to an abrupt halt, flung his arms high in the air and pitched forward, blood torrenting from a wound high in his back.

Then the stage team bolted, driven from nervousness into panic by the second burst of shooting and the louder sounds of fear from the throats of those scrambling for cover.

The sudden lunge forward scattered baggage from the roof and the driver was almost sent crashing to the street, but managed to cling to a rail where he had been crouching, ready to unload the satchels and carbetbags of his disembarking passengers.

Cuchillo grunted his dismay and almost abandoned his initial plan as he came to a halt by the rifle rack and stared out at the scene of panic beyond the law office window.

For Pinner had not run for cover when the first shots were fired. Instead, he had shoved the woman to the ground and crouched down, struggling to unbutton his holster flap and draw his Army Colt. He was between the bank and the woman, and the big rear wheel of the Concord provided him with some kind of cover. The team abruptly bolted, however, leaving the captain completely exposed, and in danger of being blasted to death by a man other than Cuchillo Oro.

For that moment, the Apache thought about lunging for the doorway, drawing the knife from under his shirt and hurling it across the street. But then the immediate danger was gone. The brake blocks of the Concord were tight against the rims, and so the wheels were dragged instead of being turned under the bulk of the stage. A great cloud of dust was raised and then billowed across the street by the slipstream of the moving vehicle.

So Cuchillo no longer had a target.

More gunshots, sounding less shockingly loud through the confusion of thudding hooves, snorting horses and creaking Concord timbers.

The Apache whirled again toward the rifle rack and allowed relief to whistle out between his clenched teeth as the right key slid into the padlock and turned the mechanism.

There were six Henry repeater rifles in the rack. Then only five. He worked the lever action of the rifle and smiled briefly when he heard a shell enter the breech.

He reached the doorway as the dust settled. The only casualties in sight were the man slumped over the sill of the broken window at the bank and the one sprawled face down in the center of the street.

Pinner was in a half-crouch now, his revolver abandoned and his arched back toward the bank as he lifted the unmoving form of the woman up into his arms. On his face was a look of depthless anguish, which the Apache had never seen there before.

A revolver shot cracked, from the livery stable next door to the law office.

"Sonofabitch!" a familiar voice snarled from inside the bank.

"Surrender, you men!" Sheriff Carson yelled, as Cuchillo identified one of the men in the bank as his principal tormentor at the Conquistador. He made this identification from the shouted curse. Then recognized the pockmarked face of Farley, framed by the jagged shards of glass still imbedded in the putty of one of the bank's broken windows.

The Apache had the Henry stock up against his shoulder by then, and was about to line up the sights on his chosen target, when Pinner straightened and turned to carry the unconscious woman into the stagecoach depot.

Time seemed to stand still in utter silence as the mind of the Indian was abruptly filled by the image of an ancient shaman named Black Cave, who had told of a dream. Then it was gone as Cuchillo rasped a White Eyes obscenity, dismissing Apache mysticism with the cold logic taught him by his American teacher, John Hedges.

Two men blasted bullets out of a window of the bank, aiming at the livery stable to drive Carson back into cover.

Boyd Farley took careful aim with his Remington at Pinner and the captain came to an abrupt halt, as defenseless as the unconscious woman in his arms.

While he had been forced to recall the dream of Black Cave, Cuchillo had allowed the aim of his rifle to wander, so that the muzzle of the Henry was now closer to drawing a bead on Farley than Pinner. He swung the weapon another fraction of an inch to the right and squeezed the trigger. The shot sounded in a brief sliver of time between a cease fire from the bank and a burst of reports from the lawman's gun. But Cuchillo knew it was his bullet that killed Farley, exploding a welter of blood from the entry wound in his cheek. Carson's shots were wild, pocking the door and sign above it.

Farley dropped from sight, an expression of surprise rather than pain on his crimson face.

"Jesus, Farley's bought it!" Brookes yelled.

Pinner had continued to stand with the woman in his arms, as if his feet were rooted in the arid dirt of the street, until the red-haired gunman's words rang out. Then he lunged toward the cover of the stage depot doorway, moving with the abruptness of something jerked by a length of rope in a powerful hand.

Bitter anguish contorted the Apache's features as he realized how stupid he had been. But there was no time now to reflect on past action.

"And the rest of you will go the same way unless you give up!" Carson shouted across the street, the excitement of impending triumph putting a shrill edge on his voice.

Pinner plunged through the open doorway of the depot, having to turn slightly to avoid crashing the head of the woman against the jamb.

Cuchillo used precious moments replacing the rifle in the rack, snapping the padlock shut and tossing the keys on the desk. Then he ran from the law office, swinging into a sharp turn to the right, then another turn into the alley beside the church.

"You don't have a chance." Carson shouted.

Cuchillo reached the total cover of the rear of the church and came to a halt, slumping down and drawing in deep breaths of the warm air of morning. As he sat there on his haunches, his back against the church wall, he felt drained. He was prepared to admit that his idleness and heavy drinking at the Conquistador were partly responsible for the tightness across his broad chest. But the run had been short so he knew the near exhaustion, which had taken a temporary grip upon him, was rooted in something more than physical effort. It was an example of what John Hedges used to call "mind over matter."

The Apache was sick in spirit and this had acted to sap the energy from his body. Only once before had he had a better opportunity to kill the hated Pinner. On that occasion he had wasted too much time in brutally toying with his old enemy. Today, he had wasted time and opportunity again in recalling the vision of a crazy old man. A vision in which Pinner had been seen with a woman at his side—but a woman with a child in her arms. Pinner's child.

More gunfire exploded out on the street, the shots coming from many directions. Men shouted, their words indistinct behind the barrage. Then came an interlude, and Carson bellowed, "Hold your fire, you people! I think they've got the message!"

"Okay, okay!" Polk shrieked. "We're comin' out! Here's our guns! Don't shoot!"

Cuchillo's bad time was over. He was able to stand up straight without effort and to feel disgust at the tacky sweat, which coated his face and pasted his clothing to his body, knowing that tension rather than exertion had opened up his pores.

He moved off, across the back lots of the buildings on the north side of Center Street, in no danger of being seen even when he had to venture into the open on the cross streets. For every citizen of Tyler Creek was converging on the area in front of the bank. His mind was still assaulted by bitter thoughts of regret, and it was with a start of unpleasant surprise that he found himself at the side of the Conquistador, in front of which the bolting team of horses had finally been brought to a halt.

The driver had run to join the large crowd outside the bank and merged with it just as a raucous cheer went up. With every man, woman, and child of the town in the throng it was impossible for the Apache to pick out individuals. But the voice of Sheriff Carson was clearly identifiable as he yelled, "Quit it! You people stop that hollering, will you!"

The noise died down and the anger of the lawman's tone sounded very distinctly along the length of the street. "That's better! We may have saved a few lousy dollars from being stolen, but we've got two of our own dead! To my mind, that's no cause for a celebration!"

Cuchillo ran from the corner of the cantina to the entrance, shielded from view by the stalled stage with sweat-lathered horses in the traces. The familiar rancid smells assaulted his nostrils. The place was empty of Cabello and customers, and he was able to take his time in crossing the barroom and going through the bead curtain.

The room that had been his sleeping quarters for three weeks no longer offered him sanctuary. But, off the kitchen was a storeroom, dusty and unused for a long time, and only slightly smaller than the room. He commandeered this for his bolt hole for two reasons. Firstly, there was no reason for Cabello ever to open the door onto it. Secondly, one of its walls was shared with the barroom and acted as a sounding board for the noise on the other side.

He squatted down, his back to the party wall, and grinned into the pitch darkness, unconcerned that the dust he had raised on entry was settling onto his sheened face and sticking there. Perhaps he had not been thinking consciously of a destination when he moved from the church to the cantina, the processes of his mind hampered by the conflicting logics of an Apache bloodline and White Eyes' teachings.

But his guile as an Indian brave had led him automatically along the right path to a place where he would have an excellent chance to discover the plans of his enemy—and then, in complete safety, be able to devise a counterplan of his own. Relishing his position, he licked the salt sweat off his lips and felt grit between his teeth. He spit saliva on the floor and broadened his grin.

"For chance to kill Pinner," he rasped softly in English, "this is one Apache who does not mind biting dust."

CHAPTER FOUR

An hour elapsed before anyone reentered the Conquistador, and during that time the heat built up inside the closet between the kitchen and the barroom. Cuchillo Oro sweated and the more moisture that beaded out through his pores, the drier his throat became. But he was no stranger to discomfort and he suffered this mild brand almost gladly, accepting it as a kind of self-imposed punishment for his mistake in allowing Pinner to live.

Which was the Apache in him. In the part of his mind that John Hedges had succeeded in making white, he was confident of his ability to simply step out into the kitchen and take a dipper of water from the bowl should his need become desperate.

Then the hour of silence was gone and he heard voices: footsteps on the street, the creak of the batwing doors.

"That bastard Carson!" Cabello growled sourly. "He gets one lucky break and figures he's the greatest lawman that ever lived! He makes me sick to my lousy stomach!"

The emaciated owner of the Conquistador came around behind the bar and rattled a bottle against a glass. Cuchillo, his ear pressed hard against the party wall, even heard the gurgle of the liquor from one container into the other.

"Well, you did tell him them three gunslingers left town," Cabello's elderly English teacher countered.

"It's what the bastards told me!" came the defensive response. "What should I do when customers go outta my place? Stand on my roof and watch them till I can't see them no more? El Paso. They told me they was headin' for El Paso."

There were more than two people in the barroom. Cuchillo heard four shots of liquor poured, then a Mexican asked, "What happened in Carson's office, amigo? He didn't spend all that time just being angry at you, did he? You find out what happened over in the bank?"

There was a pause for liquor to be tossed against the backs of throats.

"I heard," Cabello growled. "The two prisoners, they're scared of bein' hung. Wouldn't stop talkin' about how it was all the idea of the one Carson killed."

In the dark, hot, dusty, dry closet Cuchillo Oro nodded his satisfaction that the Tyler Creek lawman was claiming credit for Farley's death.

"So tell us, Edward," another Mexican urged.

The skinny old man snorted. "I got a business to run. Somebody wants to buy them drinks we just had and some more to follow . . . maybe I'll figure it's part of my business to talk with my customers."

"Sure, sure," the American old-timer agreed readily. "You pour and we'll spring for them."

Glasses were filled and coins changed hands. The Apache had a mental image of the men: Cabello behind his bar and the trio of customers leaning on it at the front. They would be sipping their drinks now, maybe leaving them untouched as they listened to the thin-faced old man tell his tale.

"There were many in the office of the boastful Carson and at first it was bad for me," he began, his tone sour. "But everyone told him he had done well in spite of my wrong information and that it was not his fault the banker and the general store clerk were killed." He paused to drink. "You will buy me another?"

"Most certainly, Edward," one of the Mexicans assured eagerly. "But to hear of the bank robbery, not of the bad feeling between you and the sheriff, of which we already know."

Cabello grunted, poured himself another drink and cleared his throat. "All right. All right. Those in the office were as impatient as you. And Carson was eager to show us what a fine lawman he could be, even when he did not need a gun in his hand." He vented a short, harsh laugh. "But the one with red hair—his name is Brookes—he would have been ready to talk to a five-year-old child to save his miserable hide."

This further expression of the skinny man's disgust for the Tyler Creek sheriff drew sighs and groans from his audience. He hurried on, "Brookes just would not stop talking, even though the other man—Polk—kept threatening him. He said it was all Farley's idea. That's the one that's dead. They were bored with this town, which has no gambling and no whores. Farley wanted some excitement and because he was their leader they had to do as he ordered them. In here last night, after the trouble with the redskin and after I had gone to bed, Farley told them his plan to rob the bank."

54

"What the hell happened to the Indian?" the American interrupted.

Liquor gurgled down somebody's throat. Cabello coughed. "Carson had him locked in a cell until this morning. Let him out just as the stage rolled in. He must have left town. Nobody's seen him since, far as I know."

"He didn't take his horse out of my livery," one of the Mexican's offered indifferently.

"Lose an Indian, gain a horse, that is not a bad trade, Luiz," another Mexican said, and laughed.

"The raid on the bank," the American old-timer reminded.

"It was not I who changed the subject," Cabello defended, then took up the story again, his usage of English becoming less formalized as the American side of his heritage came to the fore. "They left here real early, like they was headin' outta town. Woke me up to tell me they was goin' to El Paso. But all they did was head out on the trail down the hill and stash their horses. Then they came back up and broke into the bank through the window at the back.

"They couldn't open the safe, though. Not without blastin' powder, which they didn't have. Seems Farley pretended he knew about the bank havin' that big safe from the days when Tyler Creek looked set to be a boom town. So they waited for the banker to show with the keys. But old man Tuttle gave them an argument."

"Crazy bastard!" the American growled.

"What I think," Cabello agreed. "Reckon it's been a long time since there was enough money in that bank worth dyin' for."

"He was old and lonely," the liveryman added

miserably. "He lived only for his bank. Now he has died for it."

"They just shot him down for refusing to open the safe, Edward?"

Liquor was tossed down a throat and an empty glass thudded onto the bar top.

"No," Cabello replied tensely, and injected a tone of drama into his voice as he went on. "There is a young man who works for Tuttle—"

"Bob Reece," the American supplied.

"Yes, Reece. Always he takes a short cut to the bank across the back lots. This mornin' he saw the broken window and heard the voices of the banker and the men who were with him . . . this he told to Carson, you understand. Not the man called Brookes."

"We figured that out for ourselves," the American growled.

"The boy, Reece, he is feeling bad," Cabello went on, subdued and once more speaking English like a Mexican. "He blames himself for the killings because he acted the way he did. He climbed in through the broken window and tried to stop the robbery instead of going for help.

"But he was heard as he crossed the back room of the bank. Which is the office of Tuttle. They shot at him, but he was able to close and lock the door. And to shout that he would kill anyone who tried to open it. Brookes said that this was when Farley shot the banker in a mad-dog rage. The rest you know. The shooting was heard and the clerk from the general store was killed—by Farley, the red-haired man said." Cabello's tone soured again and his words dripped heavy sarcasm. "Our brave sheriff fired a lucky shot to kill the murderer and

56

the two other raiders surrendered. Somebody owes me for one more drink."

As coins clinked together in a hand, Cuchillo vented a silent sigh and began to ease away from the party wall.

But then the American old-timer asked, "How's the Dubois girl? Did she get hit?"

The Apache's interest abruptly deepened and in the hot darkness of the closetlike store room his face became set in an expression of hard concentration.

"She passed out from fear is all," Cabello answered indifferently. "She'll be fine for the weddin'."

"Wedding, Edward?" somebody asked.

"The day after tomorrow, Pablo," Luiz supplied. "It will be a big occasion for this town. Surely you know of Caroline Dubois?"

"I have never heard of her or seen her before today."

"Hey, that's right," the American muttered. "Pablo didn't come to this asshole of New Mexico until long after the girl run off."

"She sure got a big welcome when she got back, amigo," Pablo said, his voice on the threshold of awe.

"Her father was a widower," Cabello said quickly, as if anxious to relate another tale before anybody else claimed the privilege. "A miner who treated her like a slave. There was nobody in this town who did not hate him and feel pity for his daughter. She couldn't have been no older than fifteen when she stole his burro and rode off. Dubois was killed soon afterwards when a tunnel on his claim caved in and buried him alive. Nothing was

57

heard of Caroline for a long time. Then rumors began to reach here that she was doing well for herself in San Francisco. Then a message came that was not a rumor from Caroline herself, saying that she was engaged to a soldier—an army officer—and intended to return here to be married to him."

"Why did I not hear of this?" Pablo complained.

"Because you hear nothing," Luiz said, and laughed. "Except if the words invite you to have a drink, amigo!"

His laughter expanded and others joined in, until Cabello interrupted. "If there is drink to be bought, I will serve it. If not, there will be a further lesson for me."

There were some low mutterings of discontent, then a banging down of empty glasses on the bar top and a scraping of boot leather on the sawdust-covered floor of the cantina.

"Frank!" Cabello called, almost angrily.

"Not today from me," the American replied from close to the batwings. "You practice what I taught you yesterday. Me, I'm goin' up the street to the Mountain Dew. The Dubois girl and her beau are checked in there and I don't wanna miss out when the celebratin' gets started."

The doors were pushed open and flapped closed behind the departing patrons, creaking.

"Sonofabitch!" Cabello snarled.

Cuchillo relaxed then, positioning himself comfortably on the floor with his back against the party wall, confident he would hear if anyone else came into the Conquistador. Even now he could hear as Cabello slapped his English primer on the bar top and muttered his angry regret at not having carried out his threat to keep certain of his customers from entering his place again.

But then the Apache ignored his immediate surroundings and allowed his mind to ramble through time and space, settling on disjointed incidents connected only by their relevance to his hatred for Captain Cyrus L. Pinner.

He thought of the man here and now in Tyler Creek—staying down at the end of Center Street in the Mountain Dew Saloon, perhaps fussing over the beautiful young woman he planned to marry.

Then about another beautiful young woman. An Apache squaw named Chipeta, who had been his own wife at the Borderline Rancheria.

He thought of the ancient shaman's vision of Pinner fathering a boy child. And of the boy child Chipeta had given to him, Cuchillo Oro.

He recalled his shame when he was falsely accused of stealing the ornate dagger that now nestled at the small of his back.

He remembered the presence of Pinner in San Francisco and thought of what he had heard about Caroline Dubois being in that city.

The humiliation of his capture by Pinner, then a lieutenant, and the agony of the torture that resulted in the mutilated right hand.

The death of Chipeta and her baby son. The destruction of Fort Davidson.

His long weeks alone in the hills, learning to perform with his left hand all the skills of an Indian warrior, which he could no longer undertake with his right.

The images that crowded into his mind were no longer jumbled from different times and different places. They began to flow in smooth, chronological order as he mentally tortured himself with memories of why he was sworn to kill Pinner, and considered the many occasions when the opportunity had been presented to him and he had failed. He would always be doomed to failure, Black Cave had implied, until such time as the hated horsesoldier was married and the father of a son.

The batwing doors of the cantina creaked open and Cuchillo was abruptly plunged from futile reflection upon the past to morose contemplation of his present circumstances.

The sound of footsteps marked the progress of a man from the doorway to the bar, his tread heavy and weary.

"Buenas tardes, señor!" Cabello said brightly, his greeting revealing to Cuchillo that the greater part of a day had been spent in silent, secret thought.

His stomach rumbled confirmation of this as the newcomer growled, "Beer. A cold one." He was an American, his drawling accent placing his origins in the Deep South.

"I regret, señor," Cabello replied meekly, "that the night is not yet old enough for the beer to be cold."

The American sighed as he leaned on the bar. "Have to be as it comes then."

As the Apache placed his ear to the party wall he thought fleetingly once more of the vision of Black Cave, and grimaced. For he was an Indian who had learned much from the White Eyes, as a pupil of John Hedges and by contact with many others who did not realize they were teachers. It was as the result of such formal and unorthodox lessons that he was able to set aside the visions of an ancient shaman and act upon the reality of the situation.

The hated Pinner was here in this town with him, unmarried and without a son, presenting Cuchillo Oro with yet another opportunity too good to ignore.

On the other side of the wall, he could hear beer poured into a glass, and from there down a throat. The drinker belched loudly.

"It's wet and settles the trail dust, feller. And I guess it tastes better than horse piss. I'll take another."

"*Si*, señor. You have ridden far to reach Tyler Creek?"

"My business. Lookin' for three fellers. Names of Farley, Polk, and Brookes. Supposed to meet up with them in this place. Seen anythin' of them?"

There was a long pause, the tense silence seemingly having the power to force its way through the wall and beat against the Apache's eardrum.

"Señor?" Cabello rasped.

"You heard. And the way you look, I reckon you know my buddies. And what you know of them ain't good? Right?"

"*Si*, señor," the skinny man admitted miserably. "It has been bad here today."

"How bad?" The American's voice was soft-spoken, but heavy with menace.

"There was a raid on the bank, señor. By your friends."

"What happened?"

"One was killed, señor. By our sheriff. The other two are in jail, waiting for the circuit judge to come here."

61

"The damn fools," the American snarled. "I told Farley to wait for me to get—"

He had been thinking his angry thoughts aloud and something caused him to curtail the words.

"Señor!" Cabello gasped.

"I got a big mouth and you got big ears, feller. Now your eyes look enormous. Like they're ready to pop clean outta the sockets." The words were soft-spoken again, the menace even heavier than before.

"Please . . ." Cabello groaned.

"I still got business with two fellers in this town. Wouldn't want anyone to know about it before I get around to doin' it. So, *hasta la vista*, señor."

"No . . ." This time the single word began as a groan and—at the sound of a muted thud—trailed into a long sigh. A glass smashed to the floor and then there was a louder thud.

The heavy, weary footsteps dragged across the floor again and Cuchillo tracked the progress of the man along the bar, around the end and behind it. There was a sigh, a creak of a bone as the man stopped. A plop. A sigh again. Then he came out from behind the bar and crossed to the doors. They swung and creaked.

Silence. Except for the pattering of insects banging against the funnels of the coal-oil lamps.

Cuchillo listened to the intense stillness for a long time and knew that nothing larger than a flying insect was breathing in the barroom. Then he eased to his feet and said softly, "I think that is what is called dead silence."

CHAPTER FIVE

Standing in the hallway behind the bead curtain the Apache could no longer hear the suicidal insects against the lamps. For he was now in a position to listen to another sound—or rather a combination of other sounds—subdued by distance and yet loud enough to fill the town.

People were shouting and laughing and singing at the welcome-home party for Caroline Dubois in the Mountain Dew Saloon. Occasionally there was a burst of cheering and applause. A piano was being played in the background—a tune in quick tempo, which triggered into Cuchillo's mind a vivid memory of the man with the pockmarked face commanding him to dance the previous night.

Then Cuchillo pushed through the strands of beads and a quiet grin of satisfaction altered the lines of his face. He had killed that man and such humiliations were behind him. Soon all the restrictions of this White Eyes town would be behind him. The hated Pinner would be as dead as Farley and the freedom of the valley and the open terrain beyond would welcome back for all time the Apache Indian who belonged to it.

Cuchillo moved silently toward the batwing doors over which oozed the rising and falling sounds of the merrymaking. The night outside the Conquistador was dark, with the moon and stars hidden behind low clouds. The cloud ceiling and oppressive heat of the air threatened a flash storm.

Down at the far end of Center Street, the Mountain Dew was ablaze with lights, their glow spilling out of every window and the open doors. People moved about under and against the lights, like two-dimensional silhouette figures. The only other area of light on Center Street was halfway down on the north side, where pale patches escaped from the windows of the jailhouse cells.

Nothing moved on the street.

Cuchillo turned from the batwings and went between the chair-ringed tables to the end of the bar.

Edward Cabello lay on his back, legs splayed wide, one arm at his side and the other stretched above his head across a sprinkling of shattered glass. In death he looked even more emaciated than he had when alive. It was a knife that had killed him, thrust or perhaps thrown with great force deep into his narrow chest to penetrate his heart. The set of his lips beneath the drooping mustache suggested that his final emotion had been misery rather than pain.

The Apache's feelings were mixed as he looked away from the corpse and saw the open English primer on the bar top. Cabello had treated him better than most White Eyes and yet had used him. But there had been an affinity of sorts between the two men. Both had lost their wives and both had sought to improve themselves amid surroundings of squalor and deprivation. And, yes, Cuchillo had used the skinny old man, too.

He grunted as he experienced a mild pang of

guilt for thinking ill of this wantonly murdered old man. Then put him out of his mind as he turned away from the corpse.

"Hey, Ed! Why don't you shut up your place and come on down to the saloon, old buddy! Free booze aplenty, so you won't get nobody in . . ."

The American old-timer came to a halt on the threshold of the cantina, his hands grabbing the tops of the batwings. As his words trailed away, his toothless mouth hung open and his liquor-reddened and watery eyes gaped wide.

"You wrong," Cuchillo rasped across the barroom, seeking to swamp a rising tide of dread with a joke. "Already there is body here."

Then he whirled and the old man in the doorway made to back away from the batwings, a cry of fear emerging from his throat as a moist, strangled sound. He tripped over his own liquor-numbed feet and fell hard to the ground. Through the gap below the doors he saw the Apache's legs as Cuchillo took long strides to the curtained archway and went from sight beyond the swinging strings of beads.

The Indian made a sharp left turn into the kitchen and cursed silently at the closeness of food and drink as he went out through the unshuttered window. His movements were smooth and fluid, and continued to be so as he raced across open ground to the top of the bluff at the head of the valley. Then, slowly and cautiously, he started to climb down the cliff face through the pitch blackness of the moonless night.

Frank Dewinter's actions were hampered by reflexes numbed by liquor and fear, and some pain from his fall. He had to make three attempts to get

65

back up onto his feet, then spent a full five seconds trying to recall exactly what the Apache had said and why he should be scared. But that made his head ache and he recognized this as the first sign of a violent hangover.

He almost turned away from the cantina then, to go back to the saloon with its comforting prospects of a happy crowd of people, many of whom were drunk enough to buy him drinks. But the bottles on the shelves behind the bar in the empty cantina were closer. And he would not have to scrounge his way into their contents.

The crazy Indian was long gone. Was probably scared at being caught in the act of trying to steal a bottle himself. So Dewinter convinced himself he should go into the Conquistador, his mind conveniently overlooking the absence of Edward Cabello.

When he went around the end of the bar, his bloodshot eyes were fixed on a bottle of tequila and both his hands were reaching out to grasp it. Then he almost tripped again, as his boot smacked into the unfeeling ankle of what had been Edward Cabello.

He looked down and his jaw dropped as his eyes were drawn, like metal to a magnet, to stare at the blood-rimmed slit in the dead man's shirt front.

"The sonofabitch killed you!" he gasped. "That stinkin' injun . . ."

Fear gripped him and tightened his vocal chords. His head snapped around and his vision blurred. Then cleared. The bead curtain hung like an unmoving barrier across the archway through which Cuchillo Oro had gone from sight. Dewinter regained control of himself sufficiently to lift down two bottles of tequila before he turned and hurried between the tables to the batwings.

At the doorway he hesitated to look along the street. The noise from the Mountain Dew Saloon was as loud as ever. Center Street was as empty as when he had staggered along it to bring Cabello to the party. He guessed that Sheriff Carson would still be enjoying himself at the saloon, basking in personal glory as he celebrated his feat of preventing the bank robbery.

This offered Dewinter the whole length of the street to find a place where he could hide his booty. He elected to use a small hole against the wall of the courthouse facing west, which had once been a hornets' nest. The two bottles clinked together as he pushed them into the hole, and to his ears the sound had the sharpness and volume of a pistol shot.

Then, as he clenched his hard gums together, a gunshot did explode, closely followed by another, then another. The shooting went on—rifle fire pounding bullets against metal.

Dewinter came sharply erect and the shooting was curtailed. Utter silence descended on the town and it was as if the clouds had suddenly dropped lower, increasing the humid heat of the night trapped between earth and sky.

A door opened and running feet hit the street. Noise exploded from the saloon again, but now there was no note of merrymaking in the shouting voices.

Dewinter ran along the side of the courthouse and reached the front in time to see three men illuminated by the pale light from the jailhouse windows. One carried a rifle and two held revolvers.

They stood like carved statues for a stretched second, then aimed their guns along the street and opened fire on the crowd of men spilling out from the saloon.

The advance was halted.

The three gunmen whirled and raced down the gap between the law office and the livery stable.

The human tide, which had stalled out front of the saloon, began to surge forward again, voices raised higher than before. The dudishly clothed, handsome-faced Sheriff Carson broke to the front, his revolver out of its holster.

But the noise still came from a distance and Dewinter was close enough to hear the snorts of brutally mounted horses, and the thud of hooves as the animals were spurred into frantic gallops.

Then Carson skidded to a halt at the corner of the livery stable and sent a wild, unaimed shot down along the dark alley.

"Forget them, Sheriff!" Dewinter yelled as he ran out into the open. "The injun ain't with them and he's the one killed Ed Cabello!"

The single shot from the lawman's Colt had stilled the babble from the throats of the excited crowd behind him. The three horses had galloped far enough away by then for the old-timer's words to be heard clearly above the thud of hooves. As what he was saying registered in the minds of the silent crowd, heads swung and eyes stared at him fixedly.

"What?" Carson snarled.

"Cabello's dead! Sprawled out behind his own bar in his own cantina! Knifed in the heart looks like!"

"The Apache?" Carson demanded.

One of the men in the crowd behind him was Captain Pinner, who managed to maintain his military bearing despite the drink he had consumed and the fact that he had taken off his tunic. The stare in his green eyes was more intense than anyone else's, his attention snapping from Dewinter to Carson as the words "injun" and "Apache" were spoken.

"Yeah, Sheriff. The one that he had workin' for him. I walked into the place and found that savage standin' over Ed. Soon as he saw me, he ran like a bat outta hell."

"How long ago, Frank?"

"Minute or so is all. I was just comin' up the street to tell you when the shootin' started."

The sheriff, his bronzed face sheened with sweat, was momentarily torn between checking the jailhouse and heading for the cantina. Then he compromised by striding to the cell windows and peering inside at the open doors and the walls pitted by ricochets. He mouthed a curse and set off down the street, trailed by all except two men—Dewinter and Pinner.

When the army captain closed in on him, the old-timer looked regretfully after the group moving away from him. The need to take a drink from the stolen bottles was no longer urgent: not when a man with a look of evil in his eyes and the set of his mouth was advancing on him.

"An Indian worked here in this town, sir?" Pinner demanded, spitting out the words like they were bad-tasting pellets. He added the "sir" as an afterthought, when he saw the old man flinch away from him.

"Right, Captain."

"An Apache Indian?"

"Sure enough. Most Indians hereabouts are Apaches."

"What was his name?" Pinner snarled the question, as he might if an enlisted man were standing before him on report. Pinner saw that he had again frightened the toothless old-timer and he struggled to spread a smile across his face. "I'm sorry," he said, moderating his tone and bringing a dollar bill out of his hip pocket. "It's just that I have good reason to be interested in a lone renegade Apache, who stole something from me a long time ago. Forgive me, but do you know the name of this Indian?"

Dewinter found it easier to look at the bill in Pinner's hand than at the man's face. He shook his head. "No, sir. I don't recollect he told anyone his name. Everyone just called him redskin, or injun, or Apache."

Pinner was unperturbed as he held the bill out in front of him. "It may not matter, Mr. . . . ?"

"Dewinter, Captain."

"You will still get the money if you can tell me of anything unusual about the Apache."

"Unusual, Captain?"

"In his appearance," Pinner added, having to steel himself against showing impatience.

"He was big for an injun," Dewinter allowed after a pause for frowning thought.

Pinner began to breathe faster.

"Frank!" Carson yelled down the street from the cantina. "Come on down here!"

"What about his hands, man?" Pinner pressed home.

"Oh, yeah!" the old-timer said, showing his gums

70

in a broad grin. "One of them was bum. Had a couple of fingers missin'. And he couldn't do much with the ones that was left."

"Frank!" the sheriff yelled, anger in his tone.

Pinner vented a long sigh and thrust the money toward Dewinter. The old-timer took it, turned, and lurched into a staggering run toward the Conquistador.

"Cuchillo Oro," the army officer muttered, staring after the old man but not seeing him or the building toward which he was running.

"Cyrus, darling."

Caroline Dubois had to repeat her call and advance a further ten yards on him before Pinner heard her and turned. She was an extremely beautiful woman in her mid-twenties, with luxuriant blonde hair that fell to her shoulders, and big, round, blue eyes. Her mouth was sensuously full and she had attractively dimpled cheeks. Her party dress was an off-the-shoulder gown of white, trimmed with pink, which was cut modestly high at the neck, but clung closely to the fine curves of her upper body before it flared out from the waist. She was more than a head shorter than her fiancé.

"My sweet?" Pinner asked as he took hold of her arm and was again conscious of having to make an effort to mask his true emotions.

"The shooting? What happened? Was anybody hurt?" Her accent was cultured and sounded slightly unnatrual, as if she were constantly on guard against committing a social error.

He shook his head. "Not by the shooting, my sweet. That was the bank raiders escaping from jail. But a man was killed in the cantina. Knifed, it seems. By an Indian."

71

He had never told her of his blood feud with Cuchillo Oro, so she had no reason to suspect he was more than simply curious about the murder as they waited for Sheriff Carson to amble back along Center Street toward his office. Others moved much faster, anxious to return to the saloon.

The lawman bowed stiffly to the woman as he came to a halt. "Sorry all this had to happen on the night of your party, Miss Dubois. But it doesn't have to spoil anything for you. Or you, Captain. I'll be raising a posse to head out after the lawbreakers. Just a handful. You and the rest of the folks can just start again where you left off with the celebrating."

He touched the brim of his Stetson and continued on along the street with a new sense of purpose in his stride.

"You look tired, my sweet," Pinner said as he sensed Caroline staring hard at his profile, and he turned his head to respond to her survey. "And no wonder, after all the traveling we've done and the excitement of the party."

She nodded, but not in agreement. Rather, she realized her guess had been right. "You're going to join the posse, aren't you, Cyrus?"

"I feel it is my duty, my sweet."

"How so?"

"Apart from the sheriff, I doubt that anyone else in this town is experienced in what must be done. I am a trained soldier."

"But—"

"There is also the fact," he hurried on, "that I had a hand in the capture of the bank raiders and so have a personal interest in seeing them recaptured."

72

Caroline realized there was little use in continuing the discussion and smiled wanly to try to conceal her concern. "Also, as a soldier, it irks you that you have not seen active service for a long time?"

He smiled now, and was at his most handsome wearing such an expression. "Would you have me any other way, my sweet?"

She sighed. "You'll spare the time to walk me back to the hotel? If the chore will not bore you overmuch?"

Pinner looked hurt and Caroline vented a soft laugh and squeezed his hand.

"I'm funning with you, Cyrus. All that I would change about you is that you should have a sense of humor, darling. Come on."

She made the first move to head back for the Mountain Dew, as the sheriff emerged from the entrance, trailed by half a dozen men, who looked as if they would rather have stayed inside.

"Be obliged if you'd wait for me," Pinner said as the group of manhunters dispersed to go find their guns and horses. "Provided I can borrow a mount?"

Carson expressed surprise, then eagerness. "No problem, Captain. You come right on down to my office just as soon as you can. I'll feel a whole lot better in my mind knowing there's a man like you riding with us."

"Be my pleasure, sir," the cavalry officer muttered, and turned his head away from Carson and Caroline so that his smile of excited anticipation was unseen.

A mile northwest of Tyler Creek, Cuchillo Oro brought his rapid breathing under control, ran a hand over his face to wipe off the sweat, and formed his own handsome features into a smile. The emotion it expressed was satisfaction. For the sign he was following, tracking quarry as only an Apache could, had altered.

The frantic gallop had ended at this point and the three men had slowed their mounts to a walk. Cuchillo still had a large reserve of stamina.

He raised up from where he had been crouching on his haunches, examining the hoofprints, and peered hard across the rugged terrain shrouded with the deep darkness of the cloudy night. The smile drained off his face.

"Cuchillo will win," he growled. "For over great distance, horses with riders on backs are slower than Apache with chip on shoulder."

CHAPTER SIX

The feeling of dread he had experienced when he saw Frank Dewinter in the doorway of the Conquistador was expunged by the time Cuchillo reached the base of the bluff. For he had accepted the inevitable: the toothless old man would tell his story—the undeniable truth—and everyone in Tyler Creek would believe that Edward Cabello had been murdered by his former employee.

There would be much talk about the lone Apache who had worked at the cantina, and the hated Pinner would undoubtedly hear it and learn that the Indian concerned was his sworn enemy. This would make Cuchillo's murderous task more difficult, but was not his prime consideration as he worked his way around the foot of the bluff. He had killed before. Many times. But always with good reason, which enabled him to escape the consequences of his acts of violence.

Whether or not he would survive after ending the life of Pinner was of no interest to him. What filled him with bitterness, as he walked ankle-deep in the watercourse for which Tyler Creek was named, was the possibility of being hunted, captured and punished for a crime he had not committed.

The shooting had started then, and the fact that the reports were exploded high above him gave them a muted quality like Fourth of July firecrackers. The hoofbeats began, swelling in volume by the moment as the riders galloped their mounts down the steeply sloping trail that was the only way into and out of the town on the bluff.

Cuchillo had splashed out of the shallow creek by then and was crouched in a thicket of mesquite, at the point where the short trail joined the endless one that stretched from east to west.

The men rode by him in a cloud of billowing dust that augmented the darkness of the moonless night. But one man snapped his head around to steal a glance back up the hill, and the Apache recognized the bristled features of the red-headed Harry Brookes. Then the riders were gone, using their spurs brutally to demand the utmost speed from their mounts as they cut across the main trail to gallop up the northern slope of the valley.

Cuchillo waited until the night had swallowed them, checked to see that pursuit from the town had not yet started, and sprinted across the creek. As he ran, his mind followed up on the initial realization that had hit him when he recognized one of the bank raiders.

The red-headed man was free from jail, which had to mean that his blond partner had also escaped and was another member of the fleeing trio. The stranger who had killed Cabello had spoken of business in town, and it was logical to assume that he was the third man driving his horse hard up the hill ahead of the Apache.

In the event that the third man were not the murderer, Cuchillo was still able to justify his energy-

76

sapping sprint into open country. For by now he would be unjustly wanted for murder and had no alternative except to run and hide while he considered a course of action to counter the false accusation. His thought processes were those of a mind instilled with the teachings of a White Eyes tutor. While his actions were triggered by the instincts of an Apache brave wise in the ways of his people.

Although hampered by the many days of idleness and overindulgence at the cantina, he was nonetheless able to maintain an even pace of pursuit. For he took in account his less-than-perfect physical condition and ran within himself, his actions fluidly loping and utterly without tension. He breathed regularly and not too deeply, the rise and fall of his broad chest as measured a part of the exercise as the pacing of his legs and swinging of his arms. He never halted abruptly or spurted into speed again to check on the sign he was following. Instead, he slowed smoothly, eased down into a crouch, came upright easily, and took several strides to build to his chosen rate. When steep slopes enforced a slackening of his speed, he never fell into the trap of trying to make up for lost time on the declines.

Although as an Apache brave he could cover great distances on foot with the efficiency of a powered machine, he was still a mere human being—fueled by energy that could not be restocked except by rest and food. He was aware of this, but not disheartened by it, because he knew that horses were governed by the same laws.

Thus did he smile when he reached the mouth of a ravine where the riders had been forced to slow their mounts for fear of galloping them into the ground.

Cuchillo walked into the ravine, his clothing pasted to his body and strands of hair plastered to his face. He felt his heart beat slowly and enjoyed the easing of tension across his chest as his breathing rate eased. Outside of his own being the world seemed to be a dead and silent place. But he knew he was forcing such an impression upon his mind, for his hearing was attuned to pick up a particular sound and excluded all others. He was listening for hoofbeats. Either from ahead or behind him.

But he did allow a human voice to penetrate this barrier: "Okay, Donovan. Let it lay, will you? You know what Farley was like! If these two guys hadn't backed the crazy sonofabitch he'd have gone and done somethin' on his own!"

Cuchillo stopped dead in his tracks and caught his breath, holding it. The man who was talking was the one who had murdered Edward Cabello. And the Apache could hear the words as clearly as if the party wall in the cantina was still acting as a sounding board.

"All right, Hewitt. I've had my say. Question now is what the hell we gonna do? With two of their own dead, the people in Tyler Creek ain't just gonna sit on their butts and let bygones be bygones."

Donovan was an Irishman, who had been long enough on the new continent for a drawl to make inroads into his brogue.

Cuchillo let out his breath slowly and silently, head cocked to one side to get a bearing on the voices. A few yards ahead of him the thirty-feet-deep ravine curved to the right and narrowed. The

78

men were somewhere around the bend, the closeness of the rock walls serving to funnel their talk to the ears of the newcomer. He moved forward, taking short strides and lowering his feet cautiously to the ground. The air in the ravine abruptly seemed much hotter and damper, and the sweat stood out on his dark brown skin like droplets of warm rain. The saline taste was very strong when he licked his lips, reminding him that he had gone an entire day without water.

"I been thinkin' about that ever since I busted Polk and Brookes outta jail," Hewitt said. "It's gonna rain sometime, but who knows when? I want you to sit tight here. If the storm don't break soon, the posse'll track us all the way here."

"I reckon," Brookes said.

"Shuddup!" Hewitt commanded. "Donovan?"

"I'm listenin'."

"When they get here, you tell them you saw three fellers ride by. Headin' north. They'll see the tracks anyway."

"Then what?"

"Soon as they've taken off, break camp and ride for town. Then we gotta hope the rain comes to wash out our sign. We'll double back then and meet up with you in the church. Door out at the back is open."

"You're puttin' a lot of trust in the weather." Donovan complained.

There was the sound of a spit. "It don't have to rain! Just be best if it did. If it don't, then me and Polk and Brookes'll just have to bushwhack the posse and blast the bastards down."

There was a long silence as all the men considered this possibility. And Cuchillo became even more cautious now there were no other sounds to mask any he might make. For he was aware that the ravine might also carry sounds clearly in the other direction.

He reached the sharpest point of the curve and flattened his back to the rock, inching around it. Because of the narrowness of the ravine, the night trapped between the walls was pitch black. But, beyond the curve it broadened gradually as the ground sloped into a shallow basin. He saw shadowy figures—men and horses—against a patch of timber growing around the eastern side of the basin. The figures were lit from behind by the dimmest red glow emanated by the ashes of an old cooking fire.

Cuchillo lowered himself to the ground and began to belly forward, out of the ravine and into the basin.

"I was dealin' the cards one time," Hewitt growled at length. "Then that sonofabitch Farley took the deck. Now we gotta play the hands he dealt us."

There was a shuffling of feet and a noisy spit. Heads bobbed in agreement. The Apache started up the gentle slope of the basin, on the same side where the men were grouped, but aiming to reach the timber twenty yards to the right of them.

"You're right," Donovan said, and laughed. "Hell, what's a few more dead ones to us?"

"They make waves is all," Hewitt answered and swung up into his saddle. "But nothin' we can't handle."

Polk and Brookes climbed up astride their horses. The hooves of the animals rang loudly on the rocky surface of the basin, leaving in their wake the kind of suble sign that only an expert tracker would spot. The three riders reined in their mounts at the foot of the gentle slope just as Cuchillo reached the cover of the trees.

"Somethin'?" Donovan called.

"Got no idea how long this'll take, so you could have quite a wait at the church," Hewitt responded. "So take enough supplies. And stay in the room at the back where the parson keeps his clothes."

"The vestry," Brookes supplied.

"Smart ass!" Polk growled.

All three thudded their spurs into the flanks of the horses, and the animals snorted and spurted into a gallop. Up the northern slope of the basin and over the crest. The sounds of their progress were quickly lost behind the rugged terrain.

"Damn you, Farley," Donovan snarled, and unfastened the front of his pants.

Crouched in thick brush among the tree trunks, the Apache heard the hiss and smelled the steam as the man urinated on the fire embers to extinguish them. Next Donovan sat down with a weary sigh and the crack of a small bone. He drew a revolver, spun the cylinder to check on the load, and pushed the gun back into its holster.

Silence descended and Cuchillo Oro did battle with himself against the urge to impulsive action. He had only reached a position to eavesdrop on the talk when the discussion was almost finished. But it was obvious Donovan had been told of everything that happened in Tyler Creek. Including—surely?—the details of how Hewitt had killed Edward Cabello.

So, in the hot, moist, prestorm air of the New Mexico night, the Apache's first instinct was to close in on the lone White Eyes who sat just a few yards away from him. To make the man his prisoner and persuade him—in the Indian manner if necessary—to admit Hewitt's guilt. Thus, when the posse reached the basin, his first objective would be achieved.

But calculated thinking won out over the spur to recklessness in just a few moments. For there was no telling how soon Carson and his deputies would arrive. And, even if there was time to break down the White Eyes, would others of his kind accept as truth words that were extracted by Apache torture?

The mental battle won and the decision made, Cuchillo waited patiently in his hiding place. From the small sounds of restless movement and the frequent low-voice curses he heard, it was obvious to the Apache that Donovan was less easy in his mind.

Then, no more than fifteen minutes after Hewitt, Polk, and Brookes had ridden out of the basin, hoofbeats began to vibrate the humid night air again. The sounds told of many more than three riders, cantering along the ravine from the south.

"Damn you, Farley," Donovan said again, more forcefully than the first time, as he got to his feet.

The cadence of the advance slowed as the front riders of the posse reached the curve of the ravine and recognized it as a point of possible danger.

Cuchillo and Donovan looked intently at the mouth of the ravine as the horses were checked to a walk. Then the riders moved out into the basin, two abreast, with revolvers drawn or hands fisted around the frames of booted rifles. The men in the saddles were mere shadows against the dark, rocky background. But Pinner's uniform buttons glinted dimly in what little light there was, and Cuchillo recognized the familiar form of the tall and slim Sheriff Carson. Six other men rode into view and the Apache could put neither names nor faces to any of them.

All eight members of the posse were rigid and tense as they sat their saddles, heads swinging to left and right as their eyes raked the shadowed features of the basin and the dangerous rim that encircled it.

"Solid rock. We may have to check all over to find out which way they went, Sheriff."

The moment he recognized the hated Pinner, Cuchillo had instinctively fisted a hand around the handle of the golden knife at the base of his spine. Now, as he heard the familiar voice of his sworn enemy, he half drew the cinquedea from its resting place. But this was neither the time nor place, he realized, irrespective of his low chance of making an escape. The range was too long for either guaranteed accuracy or certain death. For even if the blade struck the area of a vital organ, would it have the velocity to penetrate deep enough?

"Hey, you guys!"

Donovan's shout caused every pair of eyes to swing toward his position in the trees. Revolvers tracked to the same point and rifles were jerked from boots.

Somebody said, "It's them!"

Somebody else squeezed the trigger of his handgun.

The single report was a sound in harshly shocking isolation for part of a second, then acted as a signal to a panicked fusillade, the deafening burst of gunfire counterpointed by cries of alarm from the posse.

Donovan and Cuchillo threw themselves full length to the ground, one with a curse and the other with a grimace of disgust, as bullets cut through foliage and thudded into trunks. Down in the basin, some men leapt from their saddles while others wheeled their horses and heeled them into retreat. Two did no more than bring their spooked mounts under control and then peer up the slope toward the timber. A lawman and a soldier.

"Cease fire!" Pinner roared across the din of thudding hooves, snorting horses and wild shots. "Cease fire, I say!"

He had a voice of authority, which was one facet of his military character that had made him renowned throughout the U.S. Cavalry as a stern disciplinarian. A man fired one more shot, and in its wake the sounds of men and horses coming under control seemed oddly muted. Pinner raked his green eyes over the scattered members of the posse and grunted his satisfaction. They were as cowed by his command as were the troopers who had the misfortune to serve under him.

"No one has fired a shot at us!" he snarled, and transferred his attention back to the timber. "You up there! Show yourself!"

"Like hell!" Donovan shouted. "I don't wanna get my head blowed off, mister!"

"It's captain!" Pinner corrected. "And you have my word there will be no further shooting unless you or others provoke it."

"I'm on my own."

"Then prove it, sir! By coming down here!"

He turned his head to look at Carson and his lips

moved in a whispered order for the lawman to be on the alert for a trick.

Donovan made a lot of noise rising from the brush and starting down the slope, his arms high above his head.

Cuchillo continued to watch Pinner, finding room in his heart and mind to admire the man as well as hate him. Once, long ago, when Cuchillo was just one of many braves living on the Border-line Rancheria and Pinner was a junior officer at nearby Fort Davidson, he had considered the man a coward. And his opinion had not altered for a long time after the murder of Chipeta and their baby son, a time when the depth of the Apache's hatred had allowed no opportunity for calm and collected thought about the man.

Then he had seen Pinner. Several times. Each time failing to achieve his aim of killing the man. Each time, too, gaining a new degree of respect for him. He was a bully, an intolerant tyrant of the worst kind. And, Cuchillo realized, he had mistakenly read such a trait as inevitably being the aspect of a coward's personality. For Captain Cyrus L. Pinner had proved his bravery on a number of occasions—in much the same way as he had handled the panic of the posse a few moments before.

Which pleased Cuchillo Oro. For to an Apache warrior there was far greater honor in killing a man of great courage than a craven coward.

"It is difficult to say who is the most stupid, sir," Pinner growled when Donovan came to a halt in front of his horse. "You, for greeting us the way you did, or these men for acting like terrified old ladies!"

85

Acrid-smelling gunsmoke continued to drift across the basin like wisps of early morning mist. Through it and the warm darkness the Apache saw Donovan as nothing more than a tall, thin man with arms that looked too long despite his height. He lowered his arms.

"First you try to pump me full of holes, now you friggin' insult me!" Donovan complained sourly. "I wanna tell you, this ain't the friendliest neck of the woods I ever been in."

"I'm Sheriff John Carson out of Tyler Creek, mister," the lawman put in, disgruntled and anxious to establish his leadership of the group. "There's been a murder and a jailbreak in town tonight and I'm leading a lawfully appointed posse. We figured you might be one of the men we're hunting. It was a mistake. But nobody got hurt."

The Tyler Creek citizens, who had leapt from their horses, were mounted again. They and the others moved into a loose-knit group behind Carson and Pinner.

"How many men you after?" Donovan growled sourly.

"Three," the sheriff said.

"Four," the officer corrected.

Carson nodded. "Yeah, four. But maybe not all riding together."

"Saw three, Sheriff," Donovan supplied, naming the man he was addressing and pointedly not looking at Pinner.

"Where? When?"

"Right here. About thirty minutes ago. Was just startin' to bed down for the night up in the timber. Heard riders comin' down the ravine like Satan himself was on their heels. Came racing outta the defile and up over there." He pointed to the northern side of the basin. "Way them guys was ridin' it didn't look like they wanted to be held up. So I didn't shout or nothin'. Probably wouldn't have heard me anyway. Then, when I see you guys, I put two and two together. Didn't expect to get no lead thrown at me, though."

"Sheriff Carson has already apologized!" Pinner snapped.

"No he ain't. Said it was a mistake, is all."

"I'm sorry," the lawman muttered.

"Accepted."

"Did you see anyone else?" Pinner demanded.

"Just the three is all."

"No Indian?"

"Indian?"

"Yes, man! An Apache Indian murdered a man in Tyler Creek this evening."

"No, sir. I didn't see no Indian."

"Let's go, Captain," Carson urged. "That half-hour start they have on us is getting longer every moment we waste here. And if the rain comes, we'll lose them for good."

Pinner sighed. "Yes, you are right." He nodded toward Donovan, who still refused to look at him. "We are much obliged to you, sir."

"My pleasure," the man on the ground growled as he turned and started back up the slope toward his night camp.

Carson heeled his horse into movement and Pinner's reluctance to stay with the posse was evident in the way he hesitated before wheeling his own mount. The other members of the posse fell in behind the front riders, some of them casting envious glances at Donovan.

The two-abreast column maintained a walking pace to the crest of the rise. Then a gallop was ordered.

Hoofbeats faded into the night.

The gunsmoke was now gone from the basin, but the ugly taint of its burning remained strong in the air.

"Fuckin' officers!" Donovan snarled as he made the sounds of breaking camp. "I figured I'd seen the last of them bastards when I got outta the army. They oughta ship all the sonsofbitches back east to get their asses shot off in the stinkin' war!"

Then his mood lightened as he began to pack his gear onto his horse. He had done what Hewitt had asked and now his part was over until the others returned to Tyler Creek. He began to whistle a Confederate marching song, then to sing the words as he mounted and rode his horse down the slope toward the ravine mouth, unwittingly revealing to an indifferent Apache where his sympathies lay in the far-off War Between the States.

"You are in fine voice," Cuchillo muttered as the rider went from sight and he rose and emerged from the trees. "Happy now. But soon you must change your tune." `

CHAPTER SEVEN

The threat of rain continued to permeate the hot air, stiflingly compressed between low sky and earth. But the only beads of moisture in evidence were those adhering to the flesh of the white man riding and the Indian following him on foot.

Donovan rode at an easy pace, no doubt recalling Hewitt's warning that it would take a long time to shake off the posse. So Cuchillo was able to keep his quarry within sight or hearing without overexerting himself. Free of tension because he was confident of this stage of his plan, the tall, broad, handsome-featured Apache was again painfully conscious of hunger and thirst. And he chided himself for passing up the opportunity to eat and drink during the long day he was hidden in the cantina.

Then he was able to appease his thirst, drinking from the creek in the cover of the mesquite while he allowed Donovan to ride up the trail into town. He allowed a full five minutes to pass before he started up the same route and paused at the top to survey the sprawl of unlit buildings. He had no idea what time it was, but guessed midnight had come and gone and that the early hours of a new day were passing into quiet history. Dawn was still a long way off, though, he sensed.

He was the sole source of movement upon the bluff as he glided smoothly on a diagonal line between the trail and the rear of the courthouse. But he was intensely conscious of the nearness of other people, all but one of them convinced he was a cold-blooded murderer. That one—Donovan—would be in the church vestry by now, as relaxed as when he had ridden to town, preparing himself for a long wait. The rest would be sleeping, many of them deeply as a result of the liquor they had drunk at the Mountain Dew celebration.

Cuchillo walked silently down the alley beside the courthouse, unaware he had almost stepped into an old hornets' nest, which now contained two bottles of stolen tequila. At the front corner of the building he halted and raked his eyes up and down the broad street, paying particular attention to the open doors and unshuttered windows of private houses. They were open for the slim possibility of catching some stray breeze, which might spring up to cool the fetid interiors. But at any one of them a man or woman could be standing, unable to sleep through the heat of the night.

He heard an occasional snore or grunt, but saw no movement. Just for a moment, he considered taking the safest course and withdrawing to encircle the town in order to reach the far side of Center Street. But the need to eat and rest overruled the cautiousness of his mind and he started forward, out of the cover of the courthouse and onto the open street. He walked with a casually measured gait, belying the high peak of readiness that was primed behind the nonchalant exterior.

He was within ten feet of the front of the church

when the door, which stood ajar, was creaked open.

"Somebody else who could not sleep?" Caroline Dubois said. "It's a hot night and a worrying one, is it not? If you know somebody riding with Sheriff . . ."

Cuchillo had been about to halt, whirl, and race for cover when the door began to open. But then the woman's voice sounded and he checked the actions and continued to advance without breaking his step. And he was only five feet away from her when she saw, through the darkness, details of his face and clothing.

Her mouth held the shape to speak the name "Carson" for just part of a second. Then her lips gaped wide to vent a scream as she became convinced she was face to face with a brutal killer.

But the Apache was already lunging into a countermove against the threat of capture. He shortened his pace to a half stride, and used the purchase of his leading foot to power a leap at the woman. His right arm curled to go around the back of her neck and his left hand swung, folded into a fist. He hit her on the side of the jaw and the only sound she made was a sharp crack as her teeth came together. Then her dress and underskirts rustled, as he placed both arms behind her and lifted her feet clear of the ground before she could collapse to the street.

He carried her into the gap between the church and the stagecoach depot, experiencing crazy moments of high elation as he acknowledged that he had the woman of the hated Pinner at his mercy. But, by the time he reached the rear corner of the church, reason had prevailed. A hostage was no part of his present plan.

He stooped and lowered her gently to the ground, then pulled up one eyelid to check that she would remain unconscious long enough for him to accomplish what he had come here for. The blue eye was fully up in its socket, glazed and unseeing. So he left her there and stepped silently up to the only door at the rear of the church. It was of thick, solid timber, studded with rusting nails. He had to place his ear to the keyhole in order to hear sounds on the other side. Small sounds—mere scratches against silence—of a man moving about.

He drew the knife from the small of his back, and continued to crouch against the door until a single, regular sound reached his eardrum. That of a man breathing easily as he adopted a relaxed attitude and waited for sleep to come.

But with the additional factor of Caroline Dubois to consider, Cuchillo Oro could not spare the time. Certain he had a correct bearing on the position of the man inside the vestry, he rose upright, placed his crippled hand on the latch, and drew in a deep, silent breath.

A large, warm droplet of rain hit him in the middle of the forehead. An arbitrary whim of nature, which he elected to accept as a signal. He pressed down on the latch, leaned his shoulder against the studded door, and lunged forward.

As the door swung inward, he retained his grip on the latch to keep it from fully opening to crash against the wall.

Donovan grunted and growled, "Hewitt?"

He sounded surprised, then vented a snarl of aggressive alarm as he saw menace in the speed of the newcomer entering the room. All the blankets of his bedroll were beneath him, so there was nothing to snag his hand on as he reached for his holstered Colt and began to jerk his back up off the bedding.

But the element of surprise continued to favor Cuchillo. The Apache was halfway from the doorway to the man before Donovan started his defensive counter. A dive carried him the rest of the way to his target. His right hand chopped downward to crack across the wrist of Donovan's gun hand. Pain forced a gasp from the white man's mouth and caused the fingers of the hand to splay wide, out of the fist they had formed around the butt of the Colt.

Then, as Cuchillo thudded hard atop Donovan, his left hand swung away from his side. In it was clutched the golden knife, angled for a killing thrust into a vital organ if the white man's actions should make this necessary.

They did not.

Donovan's gasp of pain expanded to a choked groan of agony as the Apache's right elbow slammed into his crotch at the same moment the Indian's left shoulder crashed into his chest. The greater fire of pain demanded the man double up, while the more forceful contact sprawled him full-length on his back again.

The clouds above Tyler Creek released their threat of a deluge on the town as, far to the east, thunder rumbled.

"The Indian!" Donovan croaked as sheet lightning exploded blueness across the heavens and the flash momentarily flooded the vestry with brilliant light.

93

Cuchillo's left arm swung down and terror filled the white man's eyes as, in the final split second of the brief illumination, he saw the glinting steel of the knife blade.

Donovan lifted both his hands to try to fend off what he was certain was a killing thrust. But the searing agony had broken clear of its source between his legs and was attacking every nerve-ending in his body, slowing and weakening his reflexes.

A moment before the honed point of the cinquedea's blade would have penetrated the flesh at the side of Donovan's throat, the Apache turned his wrist, and adjusted the swing of his arm. So it was his circled thumb and forefinger, with the top of the ivory handle, which made contact with the white man's flesh—slammed into the jaw instead of the throat.

After the lightning flash, both men were temporarily blinded, the pupils of their eyes not yet able to take advantage of what little light did exist in the dark room.

Cuchillo sensed the abrupt limpness of the man under him, but was not prepared to accept he was unconscious from one blow. So he arced his left hand back again and swung it a second time, to aim a side-of-the-fist punch at the same spot as before.

The sound of the contact was loud and sickening. The Apache winced as the pain traveled up his arm all the way to the shoulder. Donovan felt nothing, neither from the blow nor the effect it had of wrenching his head to the side.

"Truly that hurt me more than you, White Eyes," Cuchillo said ruefully as he straightened up from the inert form of Donovan, pushing the knife back into the belt under his shirt and lifting the Colt from the holster of the unfeeling man. "But later will be different, I think."

Only now did he become aware of the teeming rain that beat against rooftops and the arid ground, bringing with it a coolness that flooded that fetid atmosphere of the vestry and drove the stink of sweat and fear from his nostrils.

He stepped quickly outside and spared no thought to relishing the feel of the refreshing drops of pure water, which stung into his face, washing away many hours of dried sweat.

Caroline Dubois lay as he had left her behind the church, except that the first seconds of the summer storm had played havoc with her appearance. Her blonde hair was lank with water, her make-up was streaked and her white-and-pink gown was ruined by mud sprayed up by the force of the rain needling into the ground all around her.

She was as lax as a loosely filled sack of flour when the Apache picked her up and carried her into the vestry. Thunder crashed, much closer to Tyler Creek, and sheet lightning spread another split second of brilliant brightness between the sky and the earth. Rain filled the depression where the woman had lain in unconsciousness and the impressions that had been left by Cuchillo's moccasined feet. Mud trickled in to silt up the sign. Within moments of the Apache leaning against the door to close it, the only marks on the ground outside were the constantly changing ones of tiny holes in the mud caused by forcefully hurled raindrops.

Moments had piled into several minutes before Caroline Dubois and Donovan regained consciousness. At first they were aware only of their pain, which trapped their fuddled minds in the present. Then memory asserted itself and they recalled the Indian.

Cuchillo struck one of Donovan's matches and ignited the low wick of a coal-oil lamp. The dust of long disuse smelled evil. The white woman and the white man looked at each other then; slowly, fearfully, they moved their eyes to locate the Apache.

He said, "You nod when thinking straight. Then I throw more light on subject."

Although they both saw his broad mouth form into the line of a quiet smile, they were concentrating upon his dark eyes, which were totally impassive. And they were fearfully aware that the lack of expression was more menacing than the angriest of glowers could have been.

Their vocal response to his soft-spoken greeting was confined to grunts and growls filtered through the strips of rough blanket that gagged them. Their movements were also restricted by other strips of blanket, which bound their hands behind their backs and their ankles together. But rage, fear, and hatred glowed in their eyes as they stared across the full width of the small room.

Cuchillo had made them as comfortable as possible under the circumstances, sitting them upright and close together on Donovan's bedding, with their backs leaning against a wall and their shoulders supporting each other.

Cuchillo himself sat on the white man's saddle and leaned against the opposite wall, toying with the confiscated Navy Colt. The lamp was on the floor close to his feet.

It was a small room, no larger than twelve by

twelve, with a door into the church opposite the rear one. Around the walls were several metal hooks on which clerical garb had once been hung. But that was a long time ago. Dust clung to them now and spiders had spun cobwebs between many of them. The only piece of furniture left in the room was a three-legged stool in a corner. A patch of wall was whiter than its surroundings, showing where a mirror had once hung.

Cuchillo waited patiently for his prisoners to realize the futility of struggling and their attempts to voice more than muffled sounds. Which was not easy for him, because he had a vivid memory of Hewitt's plan to make use of the flash storm now raging above the town. But he knew his calm attitude was gnawing at the nerves of the White Eyes. He could see this in their eyes as other emotions were driven out of their minds by the most powerful one of all—terror.

When they became still and silent, leaning against each other and the wall, he nodded and lay the revolver on the floor beside the lamp. The dark metal of its construction gleamed dully in the dim light. Then he reached under his shirt at the small of his back and drew the knife from the waistband of his pants. The gold and jewels of its hilt gave a much more impressive display in the lamplight.

The eyes of his prisoners widened as he lay the knife beside the gun.

"My name is Cuchillo Oro," he said, paying particular attention to the woman. But she showed no sign of recognizing the name. "I tell you this should it be necessary for me to kill you. I think, perhaps, it helps the dying if you can curse the one who kills you. But I have no wish to kill you. Or to harm you anymore."

Donovan, who had a heavily stubbled, hollow-cheeked, sunken-eyed face, made sounds through his gag.

"I have not finished," the Apache said over the distorted words. "You see I have means to kill you. Now know I will do so if I must. Next I lay all my cards on table." The smile, which failed to touch his eyes, played with the line of his mouth again. "Want to make deal."

CHAPTER EIGHT

Once the preliminaries were over, the Apache wasted little time in reaching the point—the two points—of holding Caroline Dubois and Donovan his prisoners.

He looked at and spoke to the man first, telling him everything he had seen and heard about Farley, Brookes, Polk, and Hewitt. He told no lies, either directly or by omission. Donovan listened with indifferent resignation and made no sound or expression of response when Cuchillo finished.

"You know it was your friend Hewitt and not me who murdered Edward Cabello?" the Apache asked. He remained calm in face of Donovan's lack of feeling, but had to work at remaining composed when he looked at the woman and saw a struggle for understanding being enacted in her big, round eyes.

"It was unfortunate for you that you could not sleep tonight," he said. "For me, too, I thought. But not now. The man you are to marry has never spoken to you of an Apache named Cuchillo Oro?"

His reference to Pinner deepened her confusion and caused something of her former terror to be reestablished. She shook her head, the movement barely perceptible.

He told her the story Pinner had kept from her, picking up and toying with the ornate dagger, which had caused the whole brutal series of events to take place. In relating the details of a tragedy much more personal to him than the killing of the Conquistador's owner, Cuchillo's tone of voice remained unchanged.

The woman was fascinated and horrified from the first word he spoke. Then, as the story unfolded, Donovan was unable to maintain his pretense at a lack of interest. So that, by the time the Apache closed his tale—with the admission that he had killed Farley to save Pinner's life for himself to take—he had total command of his tiny audience. And he sensed, while they had listened and during the brief pause after he spoke the final word, that they believed the truth of what he had said.

Then fear clutched at their minds, as he rose to his feet and moved across the room, the cinquedea still fisted in his left hand.

"I cut blanket pieces from your mouths," he said. "Will cut nothing else if you speak softly only."

He severed the woman's gag first, and was just as gentle in slicing through the fabric tied tightly at the nape of Donovan's neck. Both of them sucked in great mouthfuls of the cool, damp air, which entered the vestry through the keyhole and around the frame of the door.

Cuchillo had reseated himself on the saddle and was resting his back against the wall when Donovan asked, "What you want with us, Apache? Seems to me like you got beefs with Hewitt and this lady's boyfriend." He seemed to have difficulty in keeping his voice down to a whisper and the effort gave his words an unnatural sound. His teeth and chin were darkly stained by the juice of chewing tobacco.

"You talked about a deal," Caroline added and her voice had a natural ring to it, the current circumstances not allowing her the presence of mind to upgrade her accent.

Cuchillo held up a single finger of his uninjured hand. "I wish to kill just one man." He tilted the finger to point at the woman and she flinched. "Your man. I will be hunted, and perhaps caught and punished for what I have done. This I accept. But I will not pay debt for another man's crime."

The sound of drumming rain, which intruded into the room from outside, acted in some strange manner to add to the conviction of the Apache's words.

"The deal," Donovan insisted, and was frightened by the loudness of the words. "You said somethin' about a deal," he added, whispering again.

Cuchillo nodded and got to his feet, pushing the knife back into its accustomed resting place and scooping up the revolver.

"I leave now and you will not know where I go. Soon, Pinner and the man of the law and the others will return." He was going to add "If they still live." But held back on this. "And Hewitt and the two who ride with him will come to this town. I do not know which will return first—the hunted or the hunters. But I do know I will be in position to see what happens. And to kill more than just one man if I do not like what I see."

He went to the door and rested his crippled hand on the latch.

"I'm prepared to sacrifice my own life to save that of the man I love!" Caroline Dubois hissed.

"And I ain't about to cross up a man like Roger Hewitt, Apache!" Donovan snarled softly through clenched teeth.

The big, broadly built Indian at the door shrugged as he pressed down the latch. "I think you both know Cuchillo Oro has spoken truth. Because I think this, I give you back your lives. You must decide how long you wish these to last. You, lady, may begin to shout for help as soon as I leave. He will not, because he has no desire to be discovered hiding in this town."

He pulled open the door and the sound of the lashing rain was abruptly much louder. The sudden rush of damp air chilled the tense atmosphere of the vestry. A clap of thunder exploded in the distant west. Sheet lightning flashed and, for the split second of its existence, made Cuchillo look like an apparition silhouetted in the frame of the open doorway. Then the light was gone and so was he.

"Best to stay quiet, ma'am," Donovan urged, endeavoring to wreath his features with a conspiratorial look. "Get the law involved and they'll run around in legal circles. Give that lousy injun plenty of time to blast your beau. My buddies'll be here soon. We'll find him and put him outta the way so quick you'll never—"

"Up your ass, you sneaky bastard!" Caroline snarled in the best tradition of San Francisco waterfront argot. "I ain't about to sit here and wait to be wasted by the likes of your friends." She formed her full, smeared lips into a large circle, sucked in a deep breath, and roared, "Help! Somebody help me! In the room in back of the church!"

Donovan attempted to stop her, lashing up with

102

his bound feet in a wild kick at her head. But she rolled to the side, evading the man, and continued to shout her pleas, her voice rising to a shrill pitch as fear of death from a new quarter took its vise-like grip on her.

Outside, moving fast down the side of the church, Cuchillo heard the first few words, then no more. For the teeming rain, which hid him, also served to mute all sounds except those of its own falling. He bared his teeth in a grimace of frustration and briefly considered backtracking to cut through the woman's bonds. But he immediately dismissed this from his mind, for the storm had been deluging its sign-obliterating rain for too long. Which meant that Hewitt, Brookes and Polk were certainly heading back for Tyler Creek, and that the posse had probably given up hope of a capture and turned for home. So it was imperative he find a secure hiding place as soon as possible.

He turned right on Center Street and began to run eastward, the needling drops of rain reducing visibility to no more than a couple of feet. But the geography of the town's main thoroughfare was firmly set in his mind.

After sixty strides he turned and vented a low grunt of satisfaction when a white picket fence appeared in front of him. The gate was open and he went up a cement walk between overgrown flower-beds to a half-glassed door. Hung on the brick wall to one side of the door was a shingle, painted with the legend: *Philip D. Adams, M.D.*

Cuchillo used the butt of the Colt to smash the stained glass panel of the door and grunted again when he heard a woman call, "Phil! Philip, what was that?"

103

The town doctor came awake groaning.

"Breaking glass, Philip! Here in the house! The storm or—"

"Go to the church, Doctor!" Cuchillo bellowed through the shard-encircled hole in the door's glass panel. "You are needed there!"

Without waiting for a response, he whirled and sprinted away from the Adams's house. He hurried through the gateway and diagonally across Center Street, feeling dangerously exposed despite the storm, conscious that at any moment a group of riders might burst through the soaking curtain to pulp him into the mud under the thudding hooves of their mounts.

When he reached the relative safety of the alley between the law office and the livery stable, he once more experienced a spark of self-satisfaction. Followed by a fond recollection of his old tutor, John Hedges, who had first interested a wild Apache youngster in the ways of the White Eyes. How often had he called upon the knowledge, academic or practical, which Hedges had instilled into his mind?

Tonight's example?

That a white doctor was honor-bound to answer a call upon his services. Was, perhaps, the only person in a whole community who could be solidly relied upon to do so.

Then all such thoughts were gone as the Apache climbed into the stable through a side window. It was pitch black inside, but he was able to locate his gelding by touch. Then he fitted its bridle and reins to the animal, but did not bother with the saddle.

Out on Center Street the teeming rain continued

to mask all other sounds. He left open the stable door, swung up across the bare back of the horse, and rode him slowly around the corner onto the cross street, which became the trail beyond the final, flanking buildings.

The storm seemed to lash at him with an intensified ferocity, as if nature were berating him for taking yet another unnecessary risk. But Cuchillo did not consider it unnecessary as he thudded his heels against the gelding's flanks to command a gallop down the slope to the main trail. Horse and rider raced blind through a never-ending wall of water, in imminent danger of a lethal meeting with a returning group of other riders. Until the storm-swollen water of Tyler Creek forced a slackening of speed. Then, on the far bank, the Apache headed his mount around to the left and was content with an easy canter along the westward trail.

He rode for something over a mile in this direction, occasionally having to soothe the urge to panic out of the mind of the gelding as thunder crashed and lightning turned night into day. Then he reined to a halt, swung to the ground, and cracked the flat of his good hand against the horse's rump. The animal snorted and plunged forward, lost to sight and hearing within a couple of seconds.

Cuchillo was off the trail in the same small segment of time, eyes cracked to slits against the rain and now welcoming the lightning. For two reasons. Firstly, so that he could get his bearings on the bluff, atop which the town was situated. Secondly, to keep the gelding running scared out into the barren New Mexico mountains.

Not that the animal would leave any sign, but at

least his absence from the livery stable would be a factor the townspeople would have to consider.

As he reached the base of the bluff and began to climb, the fading volume of the thunderclaps predicting that the storm would soon be gone from this part of the territory, Cuchillo felt little regret at the loss of the horse. It had been a poor mount, long past its prime, which had served its purpose in carrying him to Tyler Creek. And the animal and saddle had cost little enough—had probably not even been worth the Colt Dragoon revolver the Apache had exchanged for them.

Cuchillo picked his way up the steep cliff face over the same route he had used to descend after the killing of Edward Cabello. Then, at the top, he sprinted through the mud to the rear door of the Conquistador Cantina. It was locked and he felt a momentary pang of despair. For he was desperately anxious to be in familiar surroundings again, while he awaited the outcome of the course of events he had triggered and planned his response to whatever the outcome proved to be.

Then he shook his head in anger at the negative thought and moved along the rear wall of the cantina to the kitchen window. The shutters were firmly closed, perhaps as a mark of respect to the memory of the dead owner, but more likely for the practical purpose of keeping looters away. It took the Apache only a moment to insert the blade of the cinquedea into the crack, lift the fastening bar, and swing the shutters wide. In less than three seconds he had swung over the ledge and refastened the shutters.

He smelled grease, the aroma of stale coffee, the dryness of dead ashes in the stove, and the dampness of his clothing and hair. He heard rain beating at the shutters and the less forceful dripping of water to the floor.

Memories of the past crowded into his mind—of the days and nights in the cantina before the White Eyes Farley had come there to curtail an infrequent period of tranquility in the life of an Indian destined always to pay dearly for whatever brief happiness he enjoyed. The recollections were good ones, his mind voluntarily choosing to ignore the humiliations he had suffered. Instead, he recalled the ample food and the nightly drinking sessions. And the warm bed under a solid roof that had protected him from the elements.

But pleasant memories triggered immediate discomforts. Hunger was suddenly a physical pain in his belly. His throat ached for a hefty slug of fiery alcohol. His eyelids threatened to become sealed down by exhaustion. Again he shook his head violently, and this time gave vocal outlet to his self-anger with a curse in his native tongue. Then acted positively and selectively, ignoring his desire for liquor as he prepared to satisfy his need for food and sleep.

Moving with the skill of a blind man in familiar surroundings, he transferred food from the larder to the tiny storeroom. He also put a pitcher of water in there. Finally, he got a blanket from the cot in his old room and took this inside before he pulled the door closed behind him.

He stripped naked and used one side of the blanket to towel dry his solid, muscle-rippled flesh. Then he wrapped the blanket around him, dry side inward, before squatting down on his haunches to eat. Some dry biscuits, a can of beans, two slices of salt pork, a raw egg, and some preserved fruit. All this washed down with brackish, tepid water. His painfully neglected stomach welcomed the meal as though it were a feast of the most exotic dishes prepared by a skilled chef.

As he ate, being careful not to rush, the distant claps of thunder became less frequent and the beat of the rain on the roof and walls of the Conquistador gradually slackened. But the storm did not abate completely until after Cuchillo was asleep, his exertion and tension-wearied mind using the patter of drops as a soporific to nudge him out of reality's nightmare into a dreamless slumber. . . .

Until a gunshot jerked him back into awareness, his refreshed mind flooded with instant recall the moment his eyelids flicked open.

The flash storm was over. Daylight, which entered the kitchen around the shutters, managed to creep weakly into the storeroom under the door before it was totally exhausted. The Apache cleared his mind of thoughts of yesterday and concentrated all his senses on the present.

The gunshot had not been aimed at him. It had sounded from far outside the walls of the Conquistador and he had not heard the thud of the exploded bullet hitting a target.

He shrugged off the blanket and started to pull on his clothes. They were dry, but stiff against his flesh.

A man began to shout as footsteps sounded on Center Street. People were running, splashing through pools of water and mud, the once-hard packed dirt surface transformed into a clinging mire by the night storm. The shouting voice continued to reach Cuchillo's ears, but he could not discern words.

With the knife held against the small of his back by the waistband of his pants, and the Navy Colt clutched in his left hand, he let himself out of the storeroom. Early morning sunlight was dazzlingly bright in thin lines around the shutters, pleasantly dim in the kitchen. He stepped out across the hallway and into the room which had been his sleeping quarters in better times.

The man had stopped shouting now, and even before the Apache pressed one eye to the crack between the fastened shutters, he had worked out what was happening.

Although the narrowness of the gap severely restricted his view of the area immediately in front of the cantina, his range of vision widened down the length of Center Street. Thus was he able to clearly see the scene in front of the law office midway between the Conquistador and the Mountain Dew Saloon. Which confirmed that his guess had been correct.

Sheriff John Carson stood in front of his office doorway, and aligned behind him were six men as disheveled and weary as he was, not one of them having had the opportunity or time to clean up after riding back to town through the storm. All of them were armed with Henry repeater rifles and it was obvious that one of them had fired a shot to rouse the townspeople. The shouts had been to further encourage them out of their houses and toward the law office. The majority were already gathered there, nervously impatient as they waited for the stragglers to join them.

Women wearing aprons, some still clutching pots

109

or ingredients they had been using to prepare breakfast. Men who were unshaven or half-shaven, some wearing only hurriedly donned pants and undershirts not properly tucked into the waistbands. Everybody's clothing splashed with mud from running—already drying to a lighter shade as the early morning sun gave promise of the blistering heat it would deliver later in the day.

Cuchillo searched the crowd to no avail for a sight of the hated Pinner, then saw his enemy on the periphery of his vision, and had to lengthen the focus of his eye to see the man in detail. For he was standing in the doorway of the Mountain Dew, Caroline Dubois at his side. Despite the long distance involved, the Apache was able to see the ugly discoloration of a bruise on the side of the woman's jaw. And the expression of contained fury, which negated the man's handsomeness and made him appear ugly.

"All right, Sheriff!" a man called sourly from the mixed American and Mexican crowd in front of the law office. "Seems like you got the whole town here. You wanna let us know why?"

"Sure do, Dan," Carson replied, passing a hand over his brow in a gesture of bone-deep weariness. "Brought you all together here to warn you we've got trouble riding for Tyler Creek. Big trouble."

"We pay you outta taxes to handle trouble, peace officer!" a Mexican woman countered.

"And we sure didn't get no good return on our investment yesterday," an American taunted.

"Shuddup all of you and listen to the man," a member of the posse snarled. "It's all your futures that are on the line!"

Their curiosity aroused against a background of

110

their former nervousness, the crowd became ominously silent in intense concentration.

Carson nodded and cleared his throat. "The shootout yesterday was nothing compared with what I've heard is going to happen today, you people!" he announced, swinging his head from side to side to rake his bloodshot blue eyes over every frightened face arrayed before him. "Because if I don't have the help of every last one of you, before nightfall this town could be wiped off the face of this territory."

Cuchillo Oro had allowed his attention to wander away from the scene out front of the law office. Had felt the compulsion to look beyond the tense gathering to where the hated Captain Cyrus L. Pinner stood in front of the saloon entrance. The cavalry officer was also indifferent to the impending trouble for Tyler Creek, and was ignoring his bride-to-be, who stood only a foot away from him, her stance and expression angry. But her bitter emotions came nowhere close to plumbing the depths of those Pinner was experiencing. Then, despite himself, Pinner was unable to stifle a yawn.

The Apache parted his lips to reveal his teeth in an evil grin. "In a time of trouble it is not good to be weary, White Eyes horsesoldier," he murmured. "But be assured, I intend that soon you will rest in peace."

CHAPTER NINE

It was eerie. Almost as if Pinner's mind had picked up a distant echo of Cuchillo's threatening words. For abruptly he snapped scant words of explanation to Caroline Dubois, spun on his heels, and strode into the shadowed interior of the Mountain Dew Saloon. The woman did not even glance at him. Simply altered the lines of her face into an expression of deep anxiety as she listened to the explanation the sheriff was giving to the citizens of Tyler Creek.

"A stranger came to this town while my posse was out and you people were sleeping last night. A man named Sean Donovan. And if it hadn't been for an Apache Indian nobody in Tyler Creek ever gave a sweet damn about, he wouldn't be locked up in the jailhouse now. And we wouldn't have had any warning about what Donovan's buddies plan for us."

"You mean the injun who knifed Ed Cabello, Sheriff?" the toothless Frank Dewinter called.

Carson shook his head. "That Indian, mister. But he didn't kill Cabello. A guy named Roger Hewitt did that killing. The same guy who broke Brookes and Polk out of my jail last night."

Now Cuchillo was as interested in what the lawman was saying as everyone else in Tyler Creek.

"How you know this?" the Mexican called Luiz demanded.

"Shuddup and listen and he'll tell you," one of the weary posse members counseled sourly. "I told you to do that already, didn't I?"

Carson cleared his throat again. "Seems the Apache ran out of town after the killing. Figured he'd be accused. And he caught up with Hewitt and the others when they met Donovan. Ahead of the posse. Followed Donovan into town and trapped him in the vestry of the church. The way things happened, he also had to make a prisoner of Miss Caroline Dubois."

The lawman looked along the street toward where the woman stood and all eyes followed the direction of his gaze. She gave a brief nod, as if to encourage Carson to continue.

"Now the Apache didn't harm neither one of them more than was necessary to keep them quiet and make them his captives. Told them his side of things, then roused up Doc Adams to go release them. Got his horse out of the livery and hightailed it away from here."

"This Donovan feller, he just spilled his guts like—"

"Shuddup, Frank," Dewinter was ordered harshly.

"Pardon me for livin," the old-timer growled.

"No!" the deputy countered.

Carson was sweating in the heat of the sun. And found it difficult to keep his eyes open against the brightness, which attacked them from the sky

113

above and in reflection from the drying pools of rainwater on the street.

"Miss Dubois told the doc she believed the Apache and he had the presence of mind to lock Donovan in my jailhouse. Soon as I reached town at first light, I questioned him. But I can't claim any credit for getting him to open up. That's due to Captain Pinner."

He looked again toward the Mountain Dew, a grimace of distaste twisting the lines of his handsome face.

"I didn't approve of the method he used, but if anybody believes the end can justify the means on occasion, then we have to be grateful to the captain."

"Beat him up, eh?" Dewinter suggested.

"For personal reasons, which have nothing to do with the trouble due to hit this town," Carson supplied, the lines of grimace deepening into his sunbronzed flesh. "But once the prisoner began to talk, there was no stopping him. With the result that we now know a small army of men intend to attack Tyler Creek at noon today. With the intention, as I've already told you, of razing it to the ground."

Everyone listened to a silence that would have been total, had not flies buzzed angrily in the hot air.

"Why, Mr. Carson?" a Mexican woman asked in a plaintive voice.

"Because we took that vote at the start of the War Between the States and pledged Tyler Creek silver at a cut rate to help the Union cause, Señora Lopez. The raiders will be a band of Confederate guerillas who intend that this town will be the first

114

in the Southwest to pay for its allegiance to the government of President Lincoln."

There was another long pause, ended when a man growled, "Then don't expect no help from me. I voted the other way."

A babble of voices filled the air then, as heated arguments exploded in the crowd. The sour-voiced deputy yelled for order, but was ignored. Carson pushed his rifle high above his head and triggered a shot at the infinite blueness of the sky. Silence was reestablished, even the flies were provoked by the gunshot into sharing it.

"Anyone holds views that keeps them from fighting the Rebels, they're entitled to stay out of it," the lawman allowed, then hardened his tone. "But if when the shooting starts they side with the raiders, they'll be treated the same as them."

"I'm for lockin' 'em in the jail with the Reb already there, Sheriff!" Frank Dewinter yelled.

"And I'm for giving them the chance to save the town they live in, Frank," Carson argued. "On account of I figure we need every gun we can muster."

There was a yell of approval and Cuchillo raised himself from his half stoop at the shutters and backed away, a frown cutting grooves in his face as he considered what he had heard. He withdrew from the tiny bedroom, across the hallway and into the store place. He left the door open and listened to sounds that were again indistinct as he ate a breakfast comprised of what was left over from his early-hours meal.

He knew of the civil war that was raging in the eastern states of the country, but it had never concerned him. Very little had been of interest to him since the feud with the hated Pinner had erupted. So why should he allow such a thing to intrude upon his thoughts now?

His initial objective had been achieved. He was exonerated of blame for the murder of Edward Cabello. And the situation was set fair for him to take his revenge against Pinner. The man was still in this town and, like everyone else, believed the Apache had escaped deep into the mountains.

Yet he could not shake his mind free of this side issue, which should not have been any of his business. And, once he allowed admission to his mind of a thought he had at first barred, the reason for his concern was obvious.

He respected and admired Sheriff John Carson as the only White Eyes in Tyler Creek to have treated him fairly and with decency. Beyond that was the nagging suspicion that the lawman was being tricked and was unwittingly laying open his town to something even worse than a guerilla raid. But what could be worse than that?

And, even if he discovered the answer to this, how could he warn Carson without alerting Pinner to his presence in town?

"You are one crazy Apache," he chided himself with soft-voiced sourness. "More White Eyes kill each other, sooner this land given back to Indians."

As a further incentive to ignore the problems of Tyler Creek and its sheriff, he fingered the slight swelling on the back of his head, trying to spark fresh pain from the point where Carson's gun butt had hit him. Then he scowled and rasped, "You too thick-headed, Cuchillo. Only soft inside."

CHAPTER TEN

The finer side of the Apache's character—which the dedicated John Hedges had worked untiringly to develop—won out over his baser instincts. So he returned to his vantage point at the closed shutters and watched as the frightened people of Tyler Creek prepared to defend their town.

The talking had been completed while Cuchillo was eating breakfast and arguing with himself in the store room. Now the majority of the citizens had dispersed from out front of the law office. Just four men and two women stood on the muddy street in the harsh glare of the sun, the women frowning and biting their lips while the men huddled together in earnest conversation. All of them were Americans.

Elsewhere were scenes of greater animation and noise, as the citizens pledged to help Carson hurried to carry out his orders. Those who owned guns went into their houses to fetch them. Those who did not joined a line outside the hardware store, which carried a stock of rifles, carbines and handguns. Then, armed and with a fair share of ammunition, each man—either alone or with a woman—paid a short visit to the law office, presumably to receive a final instruction from Carson. For, immediately upon emerging from the office, each hastily recruited militiaman headed for an obviously predetermined position.

Several were already at their vantage points—among them the six men who had been deputized for the posse. They crouched on roofs or stood at doorways and windows, not yet having to take the precaution of remaining concealed.

Apart from the avowed Confederate sympathizers grouped on the street, there were four other apparent noncombatants within sight of the Apache. In the shade of the arched porchway of the church stood the elderly and stoop-shouldered town parson and the physically unmatched Doctor and Mrs. Adams—he short and stout, and she tall and slim. Down at the extreme end of Center Street, Captain Cyrus L. Pinner had resumed his position in front of the Mountain Dew's batwing doors. He had washed, shaved, and brushed his uniform and boots clean of mud. Thus refreshed, he appeared less weary and was able to inject a full measure of disdain into his expression of contempt as he watched the town's defenses being arranged.

Then, abruptly, he did something that made Cuchillo jerk back from the crack between the shutters. His scornful gaze ceased to roam the street at random and he stared hard at the front of the Conquistador. This, and the fact that the lines of his sun-bronzed face altered into an expression of deep anger, gave the Apache the unnerving feeling that Pinner had suddenly sensed the presence of his sworn enemy.

Then Caroline Dubois rasped, "To hell with you, future husband. I've got my answer ready."

118

Cuchillo let out his breath in a silent sigh as he placed his eye close to the crack between the shutters again. The woman's angry voice came from outside the cantina, to the right. He placed her position as in front of the Conquistador's entrance as he watched the hated Pinner stride purposefully down the length of Center Street.

"Just what do you think you are doing, Caroline?" the cavalry officer demanded as he closed within twenty yards of the cantina.

"This is my town, Cyrus," the woman replied as Pinner moved out of the Apache's range of vision. "I was born here and I intend to be married here. And I don't intend to stand idly by while a bunch of Rebel scum try to destroy it!"

"A Spencer rifle has a kick like a mule, darling," Pinner warned, struggling to defuse his anger and succeeding only in sounding patronizing. "You'll likely injure yourself more than anybody you aim at."

"I can only do my best," she replied and it sounded as if she were forcing out the words through compressed lips. "What do you intend to do, Cyrus? An army officer in Union blue paid by the government of Washington?"

There was a pause while he made a greater effort to control his true feelings. "I could do a great deal, my darling. If I were asked. But I'm afraid I've blotted my copybook with that soft-centered Carson. And I refuse to take orders from a man who has little idea how to plan and command. There are occasions when I have to suffer high-ranking fools on active military service. I do not have to do so in a civilian situation."

"F . . ." Caroline began, but bit back on the ob-

119

scenity. "Utter nonsense, Cyrus. The truth is that you are totally unconcerned with the threat to this town. Because you are consumed with desire to find and kill the Apache!"

Another pause, which this time was ended by the woman.

"So be it. As your future wife I must accept your version of the tale rather than that which the Apache told me. And I can therefore understand why you will never be fully content until you kill him. But in the present circumstances, the Indian is far away and the Rebels are coming closer. So kindly open the door of this place, Cyrus. I'd like to have some sort of protection when the raiders enter town."

There was a sigh, then the sound of nails being pried from timber as Pinner tore off the sealing bar.

With mixed feelings of elation and fear of what he might be tempted to do impulsively, Cuchillo moved quickly and silently back to his safer hiding place in the kitchen storeroom. He was sweating profusely as he eased the door closed and rested his ear to the party wall. The wettest area of skin was the palm of his left hand, which gripped the butt of the Navy Colt so tightly his knuckles ached.

Two sets of footsteps sounded an advance into the cantina's barroom. Chair-legs scraped on the sawdust-strewn floor. Clothing rustled as the couple sat down, at the table closest to the doorway.

"I don't believe that, Caroline."

"What, Cyrus?"

"That Cuchillo Oro is far away."

"Why do you say that?"

"Because I know that Indian!" His voice had taken on a harsher tone. "I know him better than any man I have ever served under or who has served under me. My training as an officer, I suppose. To be successful, it's more important to know and understand your enemy than your friend."

The woman attempted to heal the wound that had opened up between them. "I can appreciate that, Cyrus my dear."

"Whatever else that Apache may be, he's one savage who can be depended upon to keep his word. And something else that is certain about him is that he would never pass up an opportunity to kill me. So, item, he told you he would be in a position to kill you and Donovan if you didn't do as he told you. And he could not be certain of that until Sheriff Carson made his speech this morning. Item, he knew I would return to town. Item, the posse did not get back until daylight after the storm was over and no one would have been able to leave Tyler Creek without being seen."

"Then your course of action is clear, Cyrus," Caroline responded. "It is not yet nine o'clock and the raiders plan their attack for noon. You have ample time to look for him." She sounded unconcerned, then suddenly became almost tearfully anxious. "But I wish you wouldn't, my darling. Because even if the Indian is hiding in Tyler Creek, I'm sure he's not the only one. Hewitt and the two men with him planned to return and hide in the vestry. And that's the only place that was checked, Cyrus. They could have reached town in time to find out the Indian messed up that part of their plan. And could be anywhere in Tyler Creek now."

"What I told Carson, Caroline," Pinner replied. "Said he'd already thought of that. Reason he's having people go into his office is to tell them to keep an eye open for raiders already in town."

"You don't sound overly impressed, Cyrus."

"I'm not. Hewitt strikes me as a smart man, the way he broke those two friends of his out of jail. And you don't have to be a genius to be smarter than the hicks who live in this town."

"So?"

"So you're right, my dear. The way I dealt with Sean Donovan, I'm sure he didn't lie to me. Which means I have more than two hours to look around for myself."

"For the Indian?"

"Sure. But if I can flush out Hewitt and his partners, so much the better. Without inside help, the raid could be a complete disaster for the Rebels."

"You'll take care?"

"That was part of my training."

Shoes scraped the floor and clothing rustled again. There was a brief silence, then the sound of a kiss ending, and the woman sighed.

"You'll come back here before noon, Cyrus?"

"Of course."

His footballs receded and then were lost to hearing as he stepped across the threshold and out onto the street. Cuchillo felt deflation as strongly as he had experienced the earlier elation. For better than ten minutes he had been within as many yards of the man he was sworn to kill. And Pinner had been so preoccupied it would have been simple for the Apache to move out into the hallway and along to the archway hung with a beaded curtain. Where, with either the gun or the knife, a fatal wound would have been certain.

Why had he held back? Not because of Carson. Instead, because he also owed a debt to Caroline Dubois, the woman directly responsible for setting the record straight about the murder of Edward Cabello. How could he slaughter her husband-to-be in front of her eyes?

A choked cry of despair reached his ear across the barroom and through the sounding board of the party wall. "Oh, Cyrus," she gasped. "I love you so very much. How can such a wonderful man also be such a sonofabitching bastard in other ways?"

"Ain't nobody perfect, lady," Roger Hewitt said.

Caroline Dubois vented a low cry of terror.

Polk warned, "Any noise louder than that, ma'am, and you'll be a whole lot less than perfect."

"Have a hole more, really," Harry Brookes added with a brief laugh. "Spillin' blood outta that fine chest of yours."

Cuchillo felt disoriented as he recognized Hewitt's voice; he was gripped by a sense of unreality that made him think he was hearing the words only in imagination. But then the other two men added their comments and his mind was triggered into a logical thought process.

The trio had returned to Tyler Creek some time after Cuchillo and some time before the posse. Donovan was not in the vestry of the church and something about the place had aroused their suspicions. Like the Apache, they had indulged a trait of human nature and sought shelter and a place to rest up and think in familiar surroundings. Polk and Brookes knew the Conquistador from almost an entire day and night spent there. Hewitt had committed murder within its confines. They had entered while Cuchillo was sleeping and had perhaps been asleep themselves until roused by the gunshot. Then they had remained in silent hiding in the quarters of the dead Cabello, eavesdropping the same way he had.

"Step back away from the door, lady," Hewitt ordered softly. "Slow and easy. But not too slow. Don't want anyone out there on the street to see you lookin' like you just crapped your underwear from fear."

She had started to move the moment the order was given. Cuchillo heard her shoes scrape on the sawdust, just before the three men advanced into the barroom from the doorway, which opened onto the living quarters at the rear of the cantina.

"Donovan'll be real happy to hear about your soldier loverboy," Polk growled. "Always reckoned all officers were crapheads. And there he goes out to check on every other place except the one where we're at."

"What . ... what do you want?" Caroline stuttered.

"We're real happy about Donovan." Hewitt said, apparently ignoring her question. "That was a real inspiration of his. Bullshittin' your captain the way he did. Guess maybe if it was the sheriff beatin' up on him, he would never have thought of it. But snowin' a damn army officer. Wouldn't mind bettin' old Donovan figured the lumps was worth it. Want money, lady, is all."

Cuchillo listened as much to the sounds of their movement as of their voices. The woman and two of the men, including Hewitt, had gone to a front corner of the barroom, totally hidden from anyone who chanced to glance toward the facade of the Conquistador. Either Polk or Brookes had positioned himself beside the window to the right of the doorway.

"Money?" Caroline rasped.

"What the man said," Brookes supplied, telling Cuchillo that it was the blond-haired Polk who was watching the street.

"There's no money in Tyler Creek. Even if the bank raid had succeeded yesterday they wouldn't have got—"

"Ain't any here right now," Hewitt cut in, and a chair creaked as he lowered himself onto it. But the El Paso to Tucson stage is scheduled to stop over here in this jerkwater town at ten or thereabouts. And aboard her there'll be a quarter of a million dollars cash money. Payment from a guy in Texas to a guy in Arizona Territory for a herd of prime beef. Me and the boys figure to have that money, lady."

"Lot more each than we expected," Brookes added with another of his short laughs. "What with Farley gone and old Donovan outta the runnin'."

The men sounded relaxed and confident. Almost negligently lazy. But, squatting in the darkness with his ear pressed to the wall, Cuchillo could visualize the scene in the barroom and knew that even if the men looked the way they sounded, it would be a front. Probably, their eyes would reveal the lie.

"Why here in a town?" Caroline asked, her voice more under control now, but not too far back from the edge of panic. "Why not out on the open trail?"

Polk spat. "That much money'll have better than

125

the average guard, lady. And them guards'll be tense and edgy out in open country. Be dog-tired and ready to ease up a little in a nice safe town."

Caroline vented a low sound of scorn. "A nice safe town with a man with a gun on every rooftop and in every doorway?"

"Uh, uh," Hewitt muttered in agreement. "Made us a little angry with Donovan when we first heard about that. But our old buddy did set the time for the shit hittin' the fan way off. So the hicks with the guns won't be expectin' no trouble before midday. And we know exactly where everyone is."

There was a long silence, until Caroline said fearfully, "Now you're going to kill me?"

"Why should we do that, lady?"

"You've told me what you plan. I'm dangerous to you."

"Balls," Brookes growled.

"No, lady. You ain't dangerous to us at all. Unless we allowed you outta here to shoot off your mouth. Opposite, as it happens. You're somethin' we never counted on. Our ticket to safety. The local celebrity no one wants to see get hurt."

"A hostage?"

"On the button, lady."

In the darkness of the storeroom, which was relieved only by the scant sunlight entering through the crack at the foot of the door, Cuchillo Oro drew back his lips in a grin that gradually broadened until it injected some warmth into his dark eyes. His dilemma was solved. With more than a little luck he could pay his debts to both Carson and Caroline Dubois, which would leave him free to finally settle the score with the hated Pinner.

126

"Wish I knew where that injun was, Roger," Polk rasped from the window.

"Over the hill and far away, I figure," Brookes said. "That snot-nosed captain sure has got a bee in his bonnet about him, ain't he?"

Cuchillo recalled a long-ago lesson taught by John Hedges and thought, but did not speak aloud: "And soon Pinner will feel death's sting."

CHAPTER ELEVEN

Because many of the defenders of Tyler Creek were positioned at high points, scanning the surrounding country for the first sign of an attack, the town received advanced warning of the approach of the stage from El Paso.

The moment it showed as a dot far out on the trail running in from the east, a shout went up and was relayed from one man to the next until the word reached Carson in his office.

The sheriff came hurriedly out onto the street and sensed the tension like something that crackled through the air and brushed his flesh. He pulled the big watch from his vest pocket and frowned at the face.

"Reckon it's only the stage, John," the line's Tyler Creek manager called across the street from the depot.

"Sure," Carson answered. "What I figured." The relief expressed by his red-rimmed eyes gave the lie to his words. He cupped his hands around his mouth and yelled, "Relax, folks. Just the stage."

He repeated the assurance, directing the words along both stretches of Center Street, which was now crusted hard again by the heat of the sun.

Outside, the defenders of Tyler Creek felt

drained. They had started to become bored from being at their posts too early. Then the sighting of the approaching stage had sparked terror. As the tension oozed out of them like the sweat from their pores, many of the town's citizens experienced something close to nervous exhaustion.

Inside the cantina, Hewitt ended a long pause. "No sign of the lady's beau comin' back, Ward?"

"Ain't seen a hair of him for fifteen minutes," Polk replied. "Went out back of the livery then."

"Fine. On your feet, lady. And don't try no heroics. Like I told you, we fixed to hit the stage without countin' on you. So if Harry has to blast a hole in your back, it won't make no difference. Except to you."

Sweating in the stifling heat and darkness of the storeroom, Cuchillo heard the talk as clearly as ever. The sounds from outside were muffled, but he had picked up the drift and knew the stage was nearing town.

Straining every muscle against the chance of causing a sound, he eased away from the wall and slowly unfolded upright from the crouch. Then he inched open the door just wide enough to step sideways out into the kitchen. For part of a second he recalled how he had moved about in this part of the cantina earlier, unaware that others were hiding in the same building. The sweat beads pumped faster and larger from his pores, then he grimaced at the futility of reflecting upon past dangers he had survived.

With his shirt stained dark by perspiration and uncomfortably aware of salty droplets running across his face, he moved to the doorway that opened out onto the hall. He forced himself to grip the butt of the revolver with less force. He heard the thud of hooves, the rumble of turning wheels and the creak of springs in need of grease. He used these sounds of the stage's progress along Center Street to cover any slight noise he made in advancing along the hallway to the archway. He stood just far enough away from the stranded beads not to touch and sway them, in half-darkness, with a clear view of the brightly sunlit barroom.

The three men and a woman had also moved. Caroline Dubois and Harry Brookes stood to one side of the batwing doors. The red-headed man had his left forearm barred across her throat and was pressing the muzzle of a revolver against the base of her spine. Hard enough to bow her forward in an attitude that was almost erotic. He was smiling his enjoyment of holding her, and even had his right knee slightly bent and raised up into her crotch from behind. She looked terrified.

Hewitt and Polk were at the side of the doorway closest to the Apache and still Cuchillo received no detailed impression of the man in charge. For they were no more than black silhouettes against the dazzling sunlight streaming in over the top of the batwing doors.

The stage clattered closer, then was brought to a halt, the driver yelling to his team.

"What the hell's happenin' here, Carl?" a man demanded.

"Trouble comin' later!" the stage line manager supplied.

"You guys don't have to worry!" John Carson assured. "A bunch of Rebs have declared war on this town! Won't start until noon!"

There was a lower-voiced exchange of talk on

130

and around the stage. But Cuchillo made no effort to overhear what was being said. For Hewitt and Polk had stepped up to the batwings, and raised guns from where the butts had been resting on the floor. Hewitt had a Spencer repeater rifle and Polk a double-barreled shotgun. Both leveled them from the hip and used the muzzles to push open the doors.

"Be a rose between two thorns, Caroline," Brookes rasped, and the woman vented a small cry of pain and alarm as she was forced to assume a position on the threshold, flanked by Hewitt and Polk.

"Wrong, lawman!" Hewitt yelled, as the entire group moved as a single entity through the open doors. "Trouble starts now! Up to you how much!"

The threat, called loud in a tone that was flat, brought stretched seconds of shocked silence to the entire length of Center Street, broken only by the incessant buzzing of heat-wearied flies. Every man and woman snapped their heads around to stare at the tableau in front of the Conquistador entrance. And froze like people turned suddenly to stone.

Then two men atop the stage and one halfway out of an open door of the vehicle moved to retaliate.

"She'll die first!" Hewitt roared, his voice a snarl now.

The man beside the driver and the one who had ridden on the roof baggage had rifles. The one on the steps a handgun.

Carson, who had been about to go around in front of the stalled team when Hewitt first spoke, whirled and beat all three to the draw. He swung his Colt from left to right and brought it to bear on the man at the stage's door.

"If Miss Dubois dies, you're next, mister!" he snarled.

"All of you will!" Pinner added, stepping out of the shade between the jail and courthouses with his Army Colt angled up at the roof of the stage.

The three guards, with experienced eyes in youthful faces, halted their moves. And shifted their scowls away from the cantina to direct them at the lawman and the soldier.

"You aidin' and abettin' stage robbery, Sheriff?" the young guard beside the elderly driver accused.

"I'm preventing murder, mister!" Carson countered. "You've got nothing on board worth the life of that woman."

"Toss down your guns, you men!" Pinner ordered, moving out across the street, having to struggle to keep watching the stage guards as Hewitt and Polk advanced.

Brookes and his captive held back, standing just outside the batwings, which had ceased to flap.

"Do it, or I'll kill you!" Pinner yelled, his fear for the safety of the woman driving his voice to a high, keening pitch.

"The captain plans to marry Miss Dubois tomorrow," Carson encouraged, his tone taut.

"You bastards!" the guard beside the driver snarled, and tossed his rifle down at the street.

"Goddamnit to hell!" the man at the door rasped, and lifted his Colt slowly out of the holster to drop it.

The third guard surrendered his rifle without vocal comment.

"Beautiful," Brookes muttered close to the woman's ear.

"Now everyone else do the same!" Hewitt ordered. "And step out into the open where we can see you. You fellers on the stage, climb down."

Everyone in Tyler Creek was sweating. But nobody more than Hewitt and Polk as they passed the point of no return between the Conquistador and the stage. For they were now totally exposed to the threat of murderous gunfire from behind, either side, and ahead. And it would only need one shot—exploded by a man with scant regard for Caroline Dubois—to unleash the slaughter.

Then the two men smiled tautly as the order was complied with. First Carson dropped his gun. Next Pinner, who watched the guards and driver climb off the stage before turning to gaze at his bride-to-be and her captor. Finally, guns were tossed down from rooftops and out of doorways and windows. Men and women stepped out of houses and stores and advanced to the front edges of roofs. And defenders who had been positioned on the cross streets showed themselves in groups at the intersections.

"Roger! Harry! Ward! Let me outta this cell!" Sean Donovan's voice was loud and yet muffled.

The Apache had no way of seeing what was happening in the glare of sun on Center Street. So he had to visualize a picture in his mind based upon the words that reached his ears.

"That's fine!" Hewitt informed. "Just like we wanted it! No one does anythin' stupid now, no one gets hurt!"

Cuchillo Oro prepared to hurt somebody. He raised his crippled right hand and rested the barrel

133

of the Navy Colt across the top of the wrist. Then lowered his head so that his left cheek nestled against his left hand, which was fisted around the revolver butt. He leaned forward slightly to push the barrel between two strands of beads, taking aim on his target.

In perspective, the cantina entrance looked narrow, and above the tops of the batwings he could not see Caroline Dubois. But he had a clear view of the head and shoulders of Harry Brookes. There was a smile of pure joy etched into the profile.

The Apache's expression was grim as he brought the gun to bear on the smiling man's ear.

He squeezed the trigger. The unfamiliar gun pulled to the left, but the range was not long enough to make any effective difference to the fatal result of the shot. A dark spot appeared just in front of Brookes' thick sideburn. The man's lips curled back further, the smile of pleasure changing into a grimace of agony. The eyelids squeezed closed, then snapped open. The dark spot that was the bullet's entry wound overflowed with a stream of red.

Then Brookes was a corpse, his nervous system spasming as he started to fall to the side, then corkscrewed to the ground.

Caroline Dubois gasped, then screamed, almost pulled to the ground herself before she was able to shrug free of the dead man's arm hooked around in front of her throat.

Sure of his kill, Cuchillo jerked the revolver out from among the beads, whirled, and ran along the hallway. Then made a sharp turn into the kitchen, sprinted across it and jerked open the shutters. He went over the ledge.

Out on the street the single gunshot from within the Conquistador cantina lacked force. But everyone recognized it for what it was and the effect was stunning. Everyone froze, in the same manner as when Hewitt had first made his presence known to the unsuspecting citizens of Tyler Creek. Then all heads turned toward the source of the sound, in time to see blood gush from the exit wound in Brookes' head, then his fall, which threatened to drag his prisoner down with him.

"Harry!" Polk cried.

"Sonofabitch!" Hewitt rasped.

"I got 'em, Sheriff!" This from Frank Dewinter, as the toothless old-timer raced out from the side of the courthouse. In his left hand was a rapidly emptying tequila bottle, pouring its contents onto the sun-baked earth as he ran. His scarlet complexion and glazed, bulging eyes showed that the other stolen bottle of liquor had not been wasted. His right hand was fisted around the butt of an ancient Colt, which exploded by accident to send a wild shot high into the air.

Instinctively, Ward Polk crouched, whirled, and squeezed one of the shotgun triggers. The scattering load had only to travel twenty feet to find human flesh. At such a short range, the myriad tiny shots tore deep into the body of the old man, shredding his clothes and erupting glistening blood over an area from his crotch to his neck. The force of the blast lifted him clear of the ground and flung him backward, trailing a spray of crimson droplets.

Flies swarmed in, hesitating only long enough to allow the final twitch of the corpse to be curtailed. By which time another man had died. The guard, who had ridden atop the baggage, was the first man on the street to recover from the double shooting. He dove for his discarded rifle, got his hands around it, and had almost thudded the stock to his shoulder before Hewitt killed him, firing from the hip to drill a bullet neatly through the center of the guard's forehead.

"Roger!" Sean Donovan screamed.

He was ignored, as perhaps the only soul in Tyler Creek who was not at that moment in danger of sudden, violent death.

For, although doomed, Hewitt and Polk were making it plain they did not intend to surrender. In total isolation in the middle of the western stretch of Center Street, they abruptly came back to back. One with a single barrel of his shotgun as yet unfired and the other with a repeater rifle. As, on every side of them, people either scurried for cover or scrambled to retrieve their weapons.

Both men wore bared-teeth expressions of hatred, totally committed to face death as the punishment for failure. While on every side of them were men and women terrified of dying.

A Mexican aimed a rifle toward Polk, who swung his shotgun and squeezed the second trigger. The reports sounded simultaneously and both men died: the Mexican with a bubbling pulp on his shoulders and the American with a hole drilled through his neck from one side to the other.

With the physical support of his partner suddenly gone, Hewitt staggered backward, which took him out of the line of fire of three bullets aimed at him, from the guns of Pinner, Carson and one of the stage guards.

Then Hewitt was down on the ground, tripping

over the body of Polk. Enraged and humiliated, the man was driven into brief insanity. He rolled over onto his belly, pushed himself up onto his knees, vented a stream of screaming obscenities, and emptied his rifle in an unaimed fusillade.

Everyone who saw and heard him knew what had happened, and were content to remain in cover or stay pressed hard to the ground until the Spencer rattled empty.

Hewitt began to laugh then, confident in his deranged mind that he had terrified the townspeople into craven submission. He hurled away the rifle and clawed for his holstered Colt.

His fingertips never touched the butt. For a volley of gunfire exploded, surrounding him with awesome sound. And more than a score of the discharged bullets found his flesh. Some imbedded deep inside him. Others went through. A few merely creased him. Three or four tore chunks of him away from the whole.

He swayed one way, then another as the lead impacted against and into him. Then he dropped down onto his knees again and managed to stretch out his arms, as if begging for the torture to end. Whether his expression supported this impression no one could say, for a curtain of blood masked his features. Finally, a stream of blood and vomit issued from his gaping mouth and he pitched forward and lay still.

Silence descended upon Tyler Creek and its corpse-littered main street. Then footsteps thudded on the hard-packed dirt. Eyes and guns raked toward the sound. But horrified eyes recognized the uniformed figure of Captain Cyrus L. Pinner racing to attend to Caroline Dubois, who was leaning drunkenly against the front wall of the Conquistador Cantina.

"Harry?" the man in the jailhouse called, the plaintiveness in his tone patently clear.

"He can't hear you, Donovan!" Carson answered as he got wearily to his feet. "It's all over. Your side lost."

"It really is over, Mr. Carson?" an elderly and shriveled Mexican woman asked. "There will be no raids against our town?"

The sheriff sighed. "All lies, señora. To fool us. There'll be no more trouble in Tyler Creek."

Squatting behind the upright sign on the roof of the cantina, Cuchillo Oro growled. "Will be more trouble, man of the law. But personal."

CHAPTER TWELVE

It was nightfall before Tyler Creek returned to some semblance of normality. The stagecoach left; the dead were removed, prepared for burial, and interred. Doc Adams dispensed preparations to calm the shattered nerves of those who could not keep from trembling as they relived in their minds the events of the terrifying morning.

Sheriff John Carson carried out an investigation designed to determine who had fired the shot that killed Harry Brookes. He came up with nothing concrete and yet was reluctant to accept Pinner's firm conviction that the Apache was responsible. So the lawman went to bed early, as did most other people in town, regretting the deaths of two fellow citizens, but content at the general outcome, and with waning curiosity about the identity of Brookes' killer.

Pinner did not bed down early. Instead, he assured himself that Caroline was settled for the night, then did some drinking in the Mountain Dew Saloon. Rye whiskey. Not much. Just enough to calm himself into a frame of mind where he could think coolly about his instinctive belief that Cuchillo Oro—"Pinner's Indian"—had been in the right place at the right time to save the life of Caroline.

The more consideration he gave to the idea, the more his conviction deepened. For although, on the surface, there seemed no reason for the Apache to do such a thing, Pinner knew his man well enough to see through and under the surface. As he had told his bride-to-be, the Apache was a man of honor. He was also an Indian who spent a great deal of time in the world of the white man, and for the most part was made to suffer for it. Thus, when a white man—or woman—showed him the smallest kindness, or did him the slightest service, he felt honor-bound to return the favor.

"Yeah, it was you, you bastard!" Pinner snarled softly.

"You say somethin', Captain?" the sleepy-eyed bartender called across the saloon.

"What? No, just thinking aloud. No more drinks. You can go to bed now. I'll just take a walk before I turn in."

Pinner finished the dregs in his glass, stood up from the table and moved through the doorway. Behind him, the bartender hurried to turn down lamp wicks and do his final cleaning chores before he left the saloon to go to his room.

Outside, the cavalry officer stood for a moment surveying the length of Center Street, its hard-packed surface and the flanking buildings lit softly by a moon, which hung directly overhead in a cloudless sky. Then he began to walk, unfastening the flat of his holster during the first few paces.

He walked slowly, breathing easily from the pleasantly warm air of the mountain night. And although his eyes moved from side to side in their sockets there was no fear in them.

Cuchillo Oro was hiding somewhere close-by. He was as sure of that as he was of his love for Caroline Dubois. He was equally certain that he had no hope of finding the Apache unless the Apache wanted to be found. For Cuchillo was skilled in such tactics and Tyler Creek, with its many derelict and abandoned buildings, was an ideal place for a man to lose himself.

So Pinner planned to draw out the Apache of the Apache's own volition. And was not afraid of dying from a sneak attack with a gun or knife. Once he would have been, for at first Cuchillo Oro had hunted his enemy in a purely Apache way: seeking to ambush and kill his victim with a total and cold-blooded lack of compuncton. But from long contact with whites, he had developed his code of honor.

Pinner smiled.

"And that'll be the death of you, Indian," he murmured.

The smile remained on his face as he reached the Conquistador Cantina, swung around, and began to head back for the Mountain Dew. His expression revealed the full measure of his confidence that he could beat the Apache in any kind of fair fight.

Cuchillo watched the uniformed figure over every easy stride of the slow walk; and never once reached for the cinquedea or the Navy Colt. For his plan was already made and he had no intention of altering it, despite this perfect opportunity that Pinner was offering him.

At the end of the walk, Pinner did not turn

around to survey the town again before he went into the Mountain Dew Saloon. And even if he had done so, he would have been too far away for Cuchillo to see that the smile had gone from his face, to be replaced by a frown .touched with anger.

For as a man and an officer, Captain Cyrus L. Pinner hated two things almost as much as he hated Cuchillo Oro—to be wrong and to enter into a strategy that proved futile.

The wedding ceremony began at ten o'clock the following morning, before a congregation of everyone in Tyler Creek with the exception of Sean Donovan and the Apache.

From his vantage point behind the sign on the cantina roof, Cuchillo watched the people gather in front of the church and then go inside. First the mixed American and Mexican guests, the men attired uncomfortably in their Sunday best suits and the women enjoying the opportunity to wear their most ornate gowns. Everyone was talking too much and smiling too broadly, as if trying too hard to make the most of this happy occasion after the terror of the previous day. When the bell began to toll in the stumpy tower, the guests filed into the church.

Then Pinner and Sheriff Carson emerged from the saloon and strolled down to the church—the captain in his full dress uniform with its mass of gold braid, spurs at his heels and saber hung from his belt; the lawman wearing the jacket, which completed his suit.

Like the guests, the bridegroom and best man were over dressed for such a hot New Mexico day and their faces were sheened with sweat by the time they reached the church. Both mopped their faces and dusted off their clothing before they stepped in through the arched porchway.

The bell continued to toll, masking the sound of a wagon's progress, until it rolled off a cross street and headed up Center Street, coming to a halt outside the saloon. It was a workaday buckboard with two padded chairs on the back. The wagon and the pair of horses pulling it were decked with white and pink ribbons. It was driven by the squint-eyed, round-shouldered Luiz, looking pompously self-important in a too-tight, obviously borrowed suit.

Caroline Dubois came out of the saloon on the arm of the short and flabby owner of the Mountain Dew, who was also the mayor of Tyler Creek. Her wedding gown was a dazzling white, her beautiful face concealed by a veil. Despite the unorthodox vehicle and need to climb aboard up a short ladder, she succeeded in making a graceful journey to the church.

Watching her, the Apache felt a sharp pang of conscience. But then she went out of sight and into the church, as the bell-ringing was curtailed and a pump organ began to play a hymn tune. And then Cuchillo recalled his own wedding day, the Apache marriage ceremony, his life with Chipeta, the birth of his son, and the brutal murder of them both.

His conscience ceased to trouble him.

He let the Navy Colt be where it rested on the roof of the cantina, and dropped down to the ground in front of the building onto a street deserted of movement, except for the winging of flies through the hot air.

143

The organ music stopped and a man began to speak, joined later by many voices. The words reached the Apache's ears as a low, indistinct mumbling. He moved along and across the street, coming to a halt at the southwest corner of the courthouse. He drew the knife from its resting place against the small of his back and fixed his gaze upon the arched porchway of the church.

It would be a fair and honorable fight in front of many witnesses. A saber against a knife, which perhaps gave Pinner the advantage. But Pinner would die. Perhaps Cuchillo would be arrested and put on trial. He was prepared for that. For many knew of the blood feud between them, in this town and elsewhere. And he would have a better chance of being acquitted if he surrendered to the consequences of his act instead of running away.

The time went quickly as he considered and reconsidered his plan. He was unaware that the organ was playing a joyful tune, its pipes bellowing out the notes of the Wedding March. But the clanging of the bell in a frenetic cadence penetrated his mind and he became tense, his heart beating faster as his stomach began to churn. He had slept not at all up on the roof of the cantina and the sunlight seemed abruptly more intense—demanding that he close his eyelids against its attack. But he shook off all such feelings, blocking his mind to the potentially fatal effects of his imagination.

Luiz hurried out of the church and stood by the ladder. Then the other guests crowded through the porchway, delving into their pockets and purses for handfuls of rice. Soon, everyone was outside, with the exception of the bride and groom. And Cuchillo did not see them emerge, his view

144

blocked by the press of people. But a cheer exploded and arms swung to hurl rice.

He waited for the noise to reach a high point and begin to fade. Then stepped out into the open and roared, "Pinner!"

He took five long strides and came to a halt in the center of the street, just ten feet away from the fringe of the crowd. His shout cut across and ended the noise. Heads turned and eyes widened, mouths gaping to utter gasps and strangled screams.

The Apache stood with his feet slightly apart, his right arm hanging loosely at his side and his left bent at the elbow, holding the glittering cinquedea out in front of him. His sweating face looked like dark-stained rock run with fresh raindrops.

Seconds linked together and formed a period of imagined time, which bore no relation to the actual. Then there was a disturbance at the center of the throng.

"No!" Caroline Pinner entreated.

But her new husband ignored her plea and burst into sight at the edge of the crowd, violently hurling aside all who stood in his way.

"I knew it!" he rasped, and was unable to control a terse laugh of elation. Then an expression akin to despair flitted over his face as he reached for a holster and failed to locate it. But he quickly recovered and drew the saber from its ornate scabbard.

The crowd fell back from either side of him. Which allowed room for Caroline and Sheriff Carson to rush forward. The woman reached him first and fisted both hands around his right forearm. The lawman stopped short and hauled his Navy Colt from the pocket of his suit jacket.

"It was him, Cyrus!" Caroline screamed. "It must have been him. You can't kill him after—"

Pinner broke free of her grip as easily as if she had been a two-year-old child. He took half a step forward.

"Hold it, the both of you!" Carson snarled. "I'll blast the first one who makes a move!"

Cuchillo was unmoved, physically and emotionally. As Pinner snatched a glance over his shoulder, the Apache said, "Between Cuchillo and horsesoldier, man of the law. He know this. I know this. Everyone else has no business in this. Except to watch. Honorable fight for honorable cause. I plan this so all can see and tell."

"You won't kill me, Carson!" Pinner raged and shifted his gaze back to the Apache.

But he was off-guard, still disconcerted by the lawman's intrusion. When his wife further surprised him by rushing at him and wrenching at the saber, she was able to tear it from his grasp. Then she hurled it with the force of anger and fear along the street. It hit the hard-packed ground forty feet away.

Cuchillo felt his own anger rise as he saw this. Then saw the woman step in front of Pinner.

"All right, mister!" she flung at him. "Is it honorable now? Against an unarmed man! And you'll have to kill me to get to him!"

Pinner vented a low roar of depthless rage and made to move—to sprint along the street and retrieve his saber. But then he was rooted to the spot as Carson rammed the muzzle of the Colt hard into the base of his spine.

"Sure I'll kill you, Captain" the sheriff corrected throatily, then looked across the shoulders of the

146

groom and bride at the Apache. "And if I kill him, I'll have to kill you, too."

Time played tricks again, lengthening in the minds of everyone the actual period that elapsed in hard, tense, sweating silence.

Cuchillo brought his rage under control by recalling the vision of Black Cave. Of Pinner with a wife and son.

"What you want, man of the law?"

"One question?"

"Ask."

"It was you who shot Brookes in the cantina?"

"Yes."

Carson nodded. "Then you can leave my town, Apache. You can go into the livery, pick any horse, any saddle, and ride out of Tyler Creek. I'll guarantee you safe passage."

"You bastard!" Pinner accused.

"Please, Cyrus, darling," Caroline pleaded.

Cuchillo hesitated only a moment, then whirled and ran to the livery, pushing the knife back into its accustomed resting place. He struggled to keep his mind clear of all thought as he selected a horse, bridle and reins and swung astride the animal bareback, afraid of an assault of self-anger that might urge him into impulsive, reckless action.

As he rode the gray gelding out into the sunlight, a sea of faces were on him. He reined his mount to a halt immediately in front of the livery.

"I accept, man of the law. Pinner, there is truce between us until your marriage produces fruit of a son. For it is written that you must father issue before you die. Cuchillo Oro tried to change destiny and failed, as all men who try must fail. But we will meet again."

147

He jerked on the reins to wheel the horse. Then brought the gelding to a rearing halt as he heard a cry of pain, a yell of triumph, and a scream of fear. He snapped his head around.

Pinner had spun, wrenched the Colt from the hand of the surprised Carson, and was pushing it out ahead of him. To draw a bead on the mounted Apache.

Death stared at Cuchillo out of the eyes of his enemy. The knuckle whitened around the trigger.

Carson and Caroline lunged out of shock. The woman crashed into his shoulder and the lawman thudded against his back. Pinner was sent into a staggering fall. The Colt exploded and the discharged bullet kicked up a divot of dusty earth twenty feet short of where Cuchillo sat his horse.

The Tyler Creek parson stepped forward and set his foot hard down on the wrist of Pinner's gun hand. Doc Adams stooped and plucked the Colt out of the man's grasp.

"Ride, Indian!" the doctor instructed, and hurled the gun in the same direction as the saber.

"I go," Cuchillo responded. "After seeing Pinner in true colors. I was mistaken. Misjudged him. He still can be coward."

"Just go, please!" Caroline shrieked, close to the edge of hysteria.

The face of the Apache spread with a broad smile as he nodded. "Yes, lady. Happy that I did not fail completely. I think that on this day there is new meaning to White Eyes custom at marriage. Today, Cuchillo Oro is best man."

**Out of the American West rides a new hero.
He rides alone . . . trusting no one.**

SPECIAL PREVIEW

*Edge is not like other western novels. In a tradition-bound
genre long dominated by the heroic cowpoke, we now have
the western anti-hero, an un-hero . . . a character seemingly
devoid of any sympathetic virtues. "A mean, sub-bitchin,'
baad-ass!" For readers who were introduced to the western via
Fran Striker's Lone Ranger tales, and who have learned about
the ways of the American West from the countless volumes
penned by Max Brand and Zane Grey, the adventures of Edge
will be quite shocking. Without question, these are the most
violent and bloody stories ever written in this field. Only two
things are certain about Edge: first, he is totally unpredicta-
ble, and has no pretense of ethics or honor . . . for him there
is no Code of the West, no Rules of the Range. Secondly, since
the first book of Edge's adventures was published by Pinnacle
in July of 1972, the sales and reader reaction have continued
to grow steadily. Edge is now a major part of the western
genre, alongside ol' Max and Zane, and Louis L'Amour. But*

Edge *will never be confused with any of 'em, because* Edge *is an original, tough hombre who defies any attempt to be cleaned up, calmed-down or made honorable. And who is to say that* Edge *may not be a realistic portrayal of our early American West? Perhaps more authentic than we know.*

George G. Gilman created *Edge* in 1971. The idea grew out of an editorial meeting in a London pub. It was, obviously, a fortunate blending of concepts between writer and editor. Up to this point Mr. Gilman's career included stints as a newspaperman, short story writer, compiler of crossword puzzles, and a few not-too-successful mysteries and police novels. With the publication in England of his first *Edge* novel, *The Loner*, Mr. Gilman's writing career took off. British readers went crazy over them, likening them to the "spaghetti westerns" of Clint Eastwood. In October, 1971, an American editor visiting the offices of New English Library in London spotted the cover of the first book on a bulletin board and asked about it. He was told it was "A cheeky Britisher's incredibly gory attempt at developing a new western series." Within a few days Pinnacle's editor had bought the series for publication in the United States. "It was," he said, "the perfect answer to the staid old westerns, which are so dull, so predictable, and so all-alike."

The first reactions to *Edge* in New York were incredulous. "Too violent!" "It's too far from the western formula, fans won't accept it." "How the hell can a British writer write about *our* American West?" But Pinnacle's editors felt they had something hot, and that the reading public was ready for it. So they published the first two *Edge* books simultaneously; *The Loner* and *Ten Grand* were issued in July 1972.

But, just *who* is Edge? We'll try to explain. His name was Josiah Hedges, a rather nondescript, even innocent, moniker for the times. Actually we meet Josiah's younger brother, Jamie Hedges, first. It is 1865, in the state of Iowa, a peaceful farmstead. The Civil War is over and young Jamie is awaiting the return of his brother, who's been five years at war. Six hundred thousand others have died, but Josiah was coming home. All would be well again. Jamie could hardly contain his excitement. He wasn't yet nineteen.

The following is an edited version of the first few chapters, as we are introduced to Josiah Hedges:

* * *

Six riders appeared in the distance, it must be Josiah! But then Jamie saw something which clouded his face, caused him to reach down and press Patch's head against his leg, giving or seeking assurance.

"Hi there, boy, you must be Joe's little brother Jamie."

He was big and mean-looking and, even though he smiled as he spoke, his crooked and tobacco-browned teeth gave his face an evil cast. But Jamie was old enough to know not to trust first impressions: and the mention of his brother's name raised the flames of excitement again.

"You know Joe? I'm expecting him. Where is he?"

"Well, boy," he drawled, shuffling his feet. "Hell, when you got bad news to give, tell it quick is how I look at things. Joe won't be coming today. Not any day. He's dead, boy."

"We didn't only come to give you the news, boy," the sergeant said. "Hardly like to bring up another matter, but you're almost a man now. Probably are a man in everything except years—living out here alone in the wilderness like you do. It's money, boy.

"Joe died in debt, you see. He didn't play much poker, but when he did there was just no stopping him."

Liar, Jamie wanted to scream at them. *Filthy rotten liar.*

"Night before he died," the sergeant continued. "Joe owed me five hundred dollars. He wanted to play me double or nothing. I didn't want to, but your brother was sure a stubborn cuss when he wanted to be."

Joe never gambled. Ma and Pa taught us both good.

"So we played a hand and Joe was unlucky." His gaze continued to be locked on Jamie's, while his discolored teeth were shown in another parody of a smile. "I wasn't worried none about the debt, boy. See, Joe told me he'd been sending money home to you regular like."

"There ain't no money on the place and you're a lying son-ofabitch. Joe never gambled. Every cent he earned went into a bank so we could do things with this place. Big things. I don't even believe Joe's dead. Get off our land."

Jamie was held erect against this oak, secured by a length of rope that bound him tightly at ankles, thighs, stomach, chest, and throat; except for his right arm left free of the bonds so that it could be raised out and the hand fastened, fingers splayed over the tree trunk by nails driven between them and bent over. But Jamie gritted his teeth and looked back at Forrest defiantly, trying desperately to conceal the twisted terror that reached his very nerve ends.

"You got your fingers and a thumb on that right hand, boy," Forrest said softly. "You also got another hand and we got lots of nails. I'll start with the thumb. I'm good. That's why they made me platoon sergeant. Your brother recommended me, boy. I don't miss. Where's the money?"

The enormous gun roared and Jamie could no longer feel anything in his right hand. But Forrest's aim was true and when the boy looked down it was just his thumb that lay in the dust, the shattered bone gleaming white against the scarlet blood pumping from the still warm flesh. Then the numbness went and white hot pain engulfed his entire arm as he screamed.

"You tell me where the money is hid, boy," Forrest said, having to raise his voice and make himself heard above the sounds of agony, but still empty of emotion.

The gun exploded into sound again and this time there was no moment of numbness as Jamie's forefinger fell to the ground.

"Don't hog it all yourself, Frank," Billy Seward shouted, drawing his revolver. "You weren't the only crack shot in the whole damn war."

"You stupid bastard," Forrest yelled as he spun around. "Don't kill him. . . ."

But the man with the whiskey bottle suddenly fired from the hip, the bullet whining past Forrest's shoulder to hit Jamie squarely between the eyes, the blood spurting from the fatal wound like red mud to mask the boy's death agony. The gasps of the other men told Forrest it was over and his Colt spoke again, the bullet smashing into the drunken man's groin. He went down hard into a sitting position, dropping his gun, splaying his legs, his hands clenching at his lower abdomen.

"Help me, Frank, my guts are running out. I didn't mean to kill him."

"But you did," Forrest said, spat full into his face and brought up his foot to kick the injured man savagely on the jaw, sending him sprawling on to his back. He looked around at the others as, their faces depicting fear, they holstered their guns. "Burn the place to the ground," he ordered with low-key fury. "If we can't get the money, Captain damn Josiah C. Hedges ain't gonna find it, either."

Joe caught his first sight of the farm and was sure it was a trick of his imagination that painted the picture hanging before his eyes. But then the gentle breeze that had been coming from the south suddenly veered and he caught the acrid stench of smoke in his nostrils, confirming that the black smudges rising lazily upwards from the wide area of darkened country ahead was actual evidence of a fire.

As he galloped toward what was now the charred remains of the Hedges farmstead, Joe looked down at the rail, recognizing in the thick dust of a long hot summer signs of the recent passage of many horses—horses with shod hoofs. As he thundered up the final length of the trail, Joe saw only two areas of movement, one around the big oak and another some yards distant, toward the smouldering ruins of the house, and as he reined his horse at the gateway he slid the twelve shot Henry repeater from its boot and leapt to the ground, firing from hip level. Only one of the evil buzz that had been tearing ferociously at dead human flesh escaped, lumbering with incensed screeches into the acrid air.

For perhaps a minute Joe stood unmoving, looking at Jamie bound to the tree. He knew it was his brother, even though his face was unrecognizable where the scavengers had ripped the flesh to the bone. He saw the right hand picked almost completely clean of flesh, as a three fingered skeleton of what it had been, still securely nailed to the tree. He took hold of Jamie's shirt front and ripped it, pressed his lips against the cold, waxy flesh of his brother's chest, letting his grief escape, not moving until his throat was pained by dry sobs and his tears were exhausted. . . .

"Jamie, our ma and pa taught us a lot out of the Good Book, but it's a long time since I felt the need to know about such things. I guess you'd know better than me what to say at a time like this. Rest easy, brother, I'll settle your score. Whoever they are and wherever they run, I'll find them and I'll kill them. I've learned some special ways of killing people and I'll avenge you good." Now Joe looked up at the sky, a bright sheet of azure cleared of smoke. "Take care of my kid brother, Lord," he said softly, and put on his hat with a gesture of finality, marking the end of his moments of graveside reverence. Then he went to the pile of blackened timber, which was the corner of what had been Jamie's bedroom. Joe used the edge of the spade to prise up the scorched floor boards. Beneath was a tin box containing every cent of the two thousand dollars Joe had sent home from the war, stacked neatly in piles of one, five, and ten dollar bills.

Only now, more than two hours since he had returned to the farmstead, did Joe cross to look at the second dead man.

The scavenging birds had again made their feast at the man-made source of blood. The dead man lay on his back, arms and legs splayed. Above the waist and below the thighs he was unmarked, the birds content to tear away his genitals and rip a gaping hole in his stomach, their talons and bills delving inside to drag out the intestines, the uneaten portions of which now trailed in the dust. . . .

Then Joe looked at the face of the dead man and his cold eyes narrowed. The man was Bob Rhett, he recalled. He had fought a drunken coward's war, his many failings covered by his platoon sergeant Frank Forrest. So they were the five men who must die . . . Frank Forrest, Billy Seward, John Scott, Hal Douglas, and Roger Bell. They were inseparable throughout the war.

Joe walked to his horse and mounted. He had not gone fifty yards before he saw a buzzard swoop down and tug at something that suddenly came free. Then it rose into the air with an ungainly flapping of wings, to find a safer place to enjoy its prize. As it wheeled away, Joe saw that swinging from its bill were the entrails of Bob Rhett.

Joe grinned for the first time that day, an expression of cold slit eyes and bared teeth that utterly lacked humor. "You never did have any guts, Rhett," he said aloud.

* * *

From this day of horror Josiah Hedges forged a new career as a killer. A killer of the worst kind, born of violence, driven by revenge. As you'll note in the preceding material, Edge often shows his grim sense of irony, a graveyard humor. Edge is not like anyone you've met in fact or fiction. He is without doubt the most cold-bloodedly violent character to ever roam the West. You'll hate him, you'll cringe at what he does, you'll wince at the explicit description of all that transpires . . . and you'll come back for more.